The Secret Forest

CHAPTER ONE

Jake couldn't sleep, he had been tossing and turning since 9 p.m. Another glance at the red digital numbers on his night stand told him it was now past midnight and reminded him he had 6 hours left until he had to get up for school. The numbers ticked by, silently goading him. He groaned inwardly and turned his pillow over again, hitting it with his fist, wishing he could sleep but knowing he wouldn't be able to.

"Jake?" His mums soft voice came through his door, she must have been up to use the bathroom. Peeking her head through the door, she saw him still awake "Darling what are you still doing awake?"

Jake couldn't answer. He couldn't put his feelings and thoughts in to words. Not words that would make any sense anyway. Although everything he wanted to say flew through his mind at lightning speed, not all in order. He desperately wanted to explain and the frustration made him angry and upset all at once, all he could do was put his head in his hands while he tried not to cry.

"Its sports day tomorrow isn't it."

His mum sat on the bed and took his hands in hers, understanding without having to hear him explain what was causing him to be awake at midnight worrying about the next day ahead. She knew, she always knew.

Jake couldn't understand the point of sports day, why it was even a thing! The noise, so much noise! People everywhere, so many different games, so many different rules, everyone shouting, cheering, talking, crowded around. It was hideous. None of it made sense and they all wanted him to "take part" He never understood it and the noise would reverberate so much until it was one long continuous high pitched painful scream, then he would realise he was the one screaming. Jakes stomach knotted in pain as he remembered the last sports day.

"I will see what I can sort out ok? I'll talk to the head. Please don't worry, you need to get some rest Jake"

She kissed him lightly on his forehead "It will be ok" She laid with him a while, he had fallen in to a deep silence. Jake felt a wave of emotions crash over him and he couldn't form any part of it.

He didn't feel any better. Mum talks to the teachers and they nod and agree when she asks for him to sit out or do something else but they seem to think its "good for him" to participate and silently pat themselves on the back, when they mistake his silence for agreement after him mum leaves and they begin trying to talk him in to joining in. His inability to disagree is taken for consent and then the public meltdowns begin, cementing even more ammunition for the bullies next taunting session. Jake knew they wanted him to be "included" and he knew if he could only get them to understand then they would change their approach but it was like having a bath plug in his throat stopping his words falling out and he was silently led to whatever activity would be an absolute torture for him.

Sleep must have come for Jake eventually because he was awoken by the jabbering sounds of his excitable younger sister Sarah. Sarah was three years younger than Jake, she was eight and for his quietness she made up with her chattering. She was always jabbering on about this and that and as different as they were, they were good friends too. Sarah understood Jake.

She was rustling around in his bedroom now looking for something

"Morning sleepy head! I'm looking for the space book, I need it for school today, can I borrow it please? I promise I won't forget it this time. You should be up already, don't you know what time it is?" Sarah bounded over, full of energy and sat on his bed, her hazel eyes sparkling and ready for the day ahead, Sarah had lots of friends, she was confident, outgoing and sure of herself.. sometimes a little too sure of herself but in a likeable way. Jake loved his sister but right now he wanted her to go away.

"You're not looking too good" Sarah commented, peering at him

"What is it? What's wrong?"

Then she remembered. The realisation and understanding settled on her face leaving her exuberance behind, replaced with concern.

"Its sports day isn't it" She was quiet for a moment " Maybe Mum can talk to the teachers and really make them listen this time so you don't have to do it, maybe you can sit in the library and work on something else, maybe.."

But Sarah was interrupted as Jake threw back the covers and ran in to his bathroom just making it in time as he vomited in to the toilet.

Sarah grinned jumping up, her happiness back on track.

"Hey Jake! Problem solved! MUM! JAKES VOMMED!"

Jake had never been so relieved to be sick. Instant day off school! He spent the morning dozing in bed, recovering from his terrible night sleep and he felt all wonky too, the nerves did that to him, it was like he had jelly legs and his energy had drained from him. Mum called it anxiety, he just knew it sucked.

By the afternoon he was feeling better and by the time Sarah came flying through the door, still not slowed down after a full day at school he was ready to sit and listen to her stories of the day.

She talked so fast sometimes without a break or only a pause to check you were still listening then she would relaunch back in to whatever story she was regaling. Mum called her the Duracell battery, This didn't make much sense to Jake, she wasn't a toy that needed batteries and not the right shape either, besides batteries ran out of energy at some point and Sarah never did but whenever she said it the adults laughed so he guessed it was meant to be funny.

"You look so much better than this morning, you're not green anymore!" Sarah grinned throwing her school bag down in his room, slightly irritating Jake because other than the now strewn school bag his room was nice and tidy

"I feel better. How was school?"

"Great! I mastered the caterpillar at last! And I did it way better than that annoying Peter who just HAS to be good at everything. I went up a level in my reading AND it was Simone's birthday so we all got a chocolate at the end of the day" She bounced over and plopped on his bed

"How was yours?"

"Good" Jake smiled "No sports day for me"

Chapter Two

Saturday morning and Jake and Sarah were at the kitchen table eating cereal while their mum Rebekah was pulling the items out of the cupboards ready to clean them. She had emptied almost half the kitchen "We need a spring clean" She'd said. That actually didn't make much sense as it had become spring about a month ago, so she was a little late but Jake didn't say that as sometimes his comments were met with a funny look, an exasperated sigh or a laugh when he wasn't even trying to be funny. So he just nodded and carried on eating his breakfast.

Rebekah stood up, her hair was the same rich auburn as Jakes, they had the same oval shaped face and light dusting of freckles across their cheeks and nose, she was tall and kind, always hugging the kids and knowing when not to hug Jake as well. Sarah was blonde but with the same freckles and shaped face too, all of them had hazel eyes.

Their Dad had died when they were very young. Jake remembered him, but Sarah didn't. For a long time, it had been hard for Sarah to understand why everybody else had a Dad and she didn't but now it was accepted by all three of them and they were a strong family unit; Mum called them the triangle as it is the strongest shape and one side can't work without the other. Dad had died in a car accident on the motorway while he was working; he used to be a lorry driver and one day he just didn't come home. Mum had a visit from the police, he was only three but he remembered them knocking at the door and mums sobs that went on for days and days afterwards; the confusion that followed and how everything had changed overnight. Jake missed his smell, his scratchy chin when he hadn't had time to shave and his gruff, warm voice. He tried not to think about it too much or he became consumed by sadness and emotions he didn't know what to do with, it made him overwhelmed and angry, so he had learned to push them down to try and control it. Sarah was only a year old at the time, Jake naturally became very protective of her and they grew up like best friends... Although at times it was her looking out for him.

"You guys, it's a lovely day out there, you should go out and get some fresh air, get some exercise. It will do you both good." Rebekah announced after looking out the window

"Ok!" Sarah was out of her seat, ready to go and have an adventure "Let's go Jake"

They made their way across the beautiful lush green field littered with little white daisies at the back of their house, leading to the forest. It was their favourite place and they went for walks there often. Jake strolled slowly, soaking up the warm May sun, the promise of summer on its way while Sarah bounced, hopped, skipped then cartwheeled across the green. They were both so different in so many ways but they worked well together. In summer Jake would lay on the grass staring up at the clouds enjoying the silence while Sarah would run around looking for butterflies and rabbits, making daisy chains, all the while chatting happily, never really needing a response.

The opening of the thick forest as they approached was like a welcome balm to Jake, he felt calmer, happier and more himself here than anywhere. He closed his eyes and listened, the sounds of the branches creaking as they slowly swayed, leaves that danced along the forest floor in the gentle wind and birds singing their song, he relaxed. Gone was the noise of the smelly cars, the confusion of school and the games in the fast paced playground that he never understood. Gone were the school bells that hurt his ears; the noise of 30 kids in a class room, harsh lights and the taunts when his meltdowns would come, when he finally had to shut them all out as his brain couldn't cope with it. Here it all made sense.

Sarah was skipping around the woods looking at different coloured mushrooms that had popped up and Jake was following the slivers of sunlight that had made its way through the thick branches when he noticed it. So quick he wasn't sure if he had seen it. Then he saw it again, a flutter of colour, a shimmer of all the colours of the rainbow all at once but gone again. It had been tiny and over by a fallen tree where a tree stump lay in a c shape. Jake walked over to it and that's when he heard it, a tinkling noise so faint it was almost a tickle to his ears... faint laughter.

"Did you hear that?"

"Hear what?" Sarah had found a circle of mushrooms now and was busy inspecting it "Isn't it strange how they make these circles like this"

"That noise" Jake continued, "It was very quiet but it was over here. It was definitely over here"

"No Jake I didn't hear anything. Are you sure you heard it?" Sarah raised an eyebrow at him

"I'm sure!"

"Ok" Sarah wasn't listening she had gone back to counting how many mushrooms were in the circle.

Jake stood still and listened, the sound had gone now but it was here, he HAD heard it. He was about to turn around when something caught his eye again, a flutter and a face, a tiny face so small, he couldn't be sure he had even seen it at all. Did he imagine it?

"What's wrong?"

"Nothing. I – I saw something"

"Ooh what did you see? A squirrel?"

"No. Nothing like that" Jake shook his head but carried on staring at the spot he had seen it, wishing it would come back

"What was it then?" Sarah persisted

"It must have been the light playing tricks. There was rainbow colours, but so quick then it was gone..and .."

"And what?"

"Looked like a face, but it couldn't be. I heard laughter. Must have been the wind." Jake concluded

"FAIRIES!" Sarah exclaimed, not containing her excitement. "That explains the mushrooms, of COURSE there are fairies here!"

"Don't be ridiculous Sarah! There are no such thing as fairies!"

"Then how do you explain what you saw and heard?"

 This did stump Jake, but he simply did not believe in such things, although he knew what he had seen, or had he? It was so quick he almost hadn't seen it. Maybe it was his imagination after all.

"Hmmmm" Sarah looked at Jake as if she knew far better than he did and pranced off among the mushrooms back to her counting. They spent hours there, inspecting the new shoots of nature, the fungi on the trees, how the roots came right out of the ground like lots of legs and spread out, criss crossing over each other. It was a beautiful place and they knew it well. It was late afternoon before they started to head back, no more talk of fairies, only their rumbling tummies and when they came through the kitchen door Jake and Sarah could smell the beautiful casserole their mum had been cooking. She had cleaned the house and was relaxing with a cup of tea when they came back.

"Hey you two, have a nice time?"

"Yep, it was great and mum guess what?" Sarah called through, taking her shoes off so as not to muddy the clean floor

"What darling?"

"There's fairies in the woods"

 Jake just rolled his eyes at his sister while Rebekah came to give them both a hug

"Is there? Oh that's nice"

CHAPTER THREE

That place between asleep and awake where
your body is at it's lightest and you remember
your dreams; where anything is possible and your
floating. She was so beautiful, like a fragile
ornament. Graceful and delicate. Her touch as
soft as a petal, her smile so warm and inviting.
Eyes full of love and light. Her voice, like tinkling
soft music. She fluttered past him, he couldn't see
her now but still sense her and he stirred "Jake,"
She breathed, it was so quiet he almost hadn't
heard it "Jake, come with me" and he went.

He was above the clouds, he didn't feel scared.
Somehow he knew he was safe, he was being
protected. Then flying past beautiful seas seeing
their immense body of water, breathing the salt
air in to his senses. He was taken over woods,
their earthy scent filling him with deep happiness,
the sounds of nature, music to his ears. Never
before had he felt so alive and free, he knew he

could wake at any moment and didn't want this feeling to ever end.

When Jake did wake, he knew he felt sure of one thing. He had to go back to the forest.

"Can I come?" Sarah was already pulling on her boots, knowing he would be going on one of his walks. Jake had tried to leave quietly (which he was pretty good at) but Sarah seemed to sense when Jake was going somewhere, and usually crashed along in all her noisy glory (Which she was pretty good at)

"Um, I just fancy a quiet walk today Sarah. Maybe tomorrow?"

"I can be quiet!" She looked offended at first, then grinned and turned in to an inspector character pretending to snoop along the halls with exaggerated slowness, tip toeing and putting her finger to her lips "See" She whispered. Jake smiled, she really was funny but if he had any chance of seeing what he thought he might see, she would have to either be completely silent or stay at home. Completely silent seemed to be out of the question for her so as mean as he felt he stuck to his guns and said no.

"Let's play a game when I get back, I just want to be on my own for this one. Sorry Sarah"

Her face fell and she looked hurt "Ok" She said suddenly becoming very quiet as she walked away. Jake felt terrible. He hardly ever went out for a walk without Sarah and he didn't think he had ever said no to her either, unless she was about to do something daft and fraught with danger like change the plug by herself because it stopped working on the downstairs TV; She was 5, Jake had walked in just when she was about to jam it open with a screwdriver. Or the time she decided it was a good idea to make breakfast for their Mum on Mother's Day and tried to heat a tin of beans in the microwave, Both times Jake found his normally quiet voice turning in to a loud "Nooooo" stopping her in her tracks.

Sarah's big personality seemed to shrink a little as she went, Jake turned and walked out the door softly before he could change his mind.

It was early, not yet 8:30. The air was fresh and full of morning dew. Birds were singing and calling to each other, the grass was slightly wet but the sun was bright and there were no clouds, it would be warm soon. Jake walked purposefully across the fields towards the woods, focusing on his dream, the sounds he heard before and the flash of colour he could not explain. He had to go back to that exact spot where the semicircle tree trunk was. He was so focused he didn't see Sarah still in stealth mode creeping along behind him, far enough so he wouldn't see her, she was in complete character with sunglasses and her dolly Betty who was the favourite at the moment who came on most of her adventures. She kept ducking down in the grass, darting her hands back and forth as if she expected an attacker at any moment and then scurrying along head bent being as quiet as Sarah could possibly manage. Once she even threw herself down on her stomach and put her hands over Betty's mouth to stop her from making a sound while she waited for Jake to continue in to the woods "Aha! " She said to Betty "I knew it"

 Jake stepped through the forest, the familiar feeling of calm washing over him instantly. It was much cooler here under the shade of the trees, quieter too. The wind was slight and it felt very still, but he heard the birds tweeting their tunes and leaves skittering across the ground occasionally. He closed his eyes, taking a deep breath and listened intently. He felt connected with the nature around him and stayed as still as he could, concentrating. At first, it was his breathing that seemed all he could hear but after a few moments he could focus on other sounds; the branches gently creaking and swishing their leaves, different calls of birds nesting above, a scurrying of a squirrel maybe and tinkling laughter, so faint it almost wasn't there. But it was there! His eyes snapped open yet he stayed deadly still, searching where it may have come from, the semicircle tree trunk was close by to his left, he was certain it had come from that direction. Jakes eyes were fixed to the spot, waiting, watching and listening when a tiny high pitched noise came from there, a flutter of colour and something shimmering. It was like a transparent rainbow making the air wobble. He stepped slowly forward to the tree trunk until he was almost on top of it, peering down, all he could see was the tree trunk, it looked like it had been cut down it was so even. There was moss growing around it and some large pebbles, twigs and roots from other trees twisted and turning over themselves nearby, but other than that there was nothing unusual. Jake heard something else, he couldn't make it out. It was so faint he struggled to even identify what sounds they were, all he knew was they were there. He leaned forward further still, the sound teasing his ears until he was bending completely over the tree trunk. Suddenly a white light flashed open in front of him and he fell. Jake expected to hit the ground in front of him and put his hands out in front of him, wincing in expectation. He had leaned over too far and lost balance. Jake waited for the impact but it didn't happen and he realised he was still falling.

When Jake landed he looked around in surprise, he wasn't hurt but he was on top of a pile of leaves. Leaves? Confused, Jake stood up and brushed himself off, he looked around and couldn't believe his eyes. He was small, smaller than small, miniscule! A leaf was bigger than him, the pile of leaves that had cushioned his fall were like a giant bed to him. The roots of the trees he was looking at earlier were four times bigger than him, the tree trunk he had been so carefully studying was enormous and loomed in front of him, he had to now lean his head back to look at it.

The most amazing thing though was what was sitting on a mushroom a little to the right of him, watching him intently with a smile on her face.

She was like a tiny porcelain doll, graceful the way she sat. Perfect posture. Wearing a shimmering purple dress that flowed with her movements, her eyes looked amused when she watched him, she had long flowing black hair and when she moved the air seemed to ripple.

"Hello Jake" She spoke softly "You found us at last"

Jake couldn't speak, he was taking it all in, she got up then. No, not got up, lifted her up was her beautiful translucent wings that held all the colours of a rainbow and she floated nearer

"I'm Raven" She stopped a little in front of him then glanced up and smiled as she looked towards the tree trunk when they both heard....

"Jake!" Sarah's voice came clear in to the forest "Jake, where are you? I know you're here, I SAW you here"

Sarah was now peering over the tree trunk just like Jake did but little did Sarah know that she was being watched by Jake who was about the size of a ladybird and Raven. Jake watched as what happened to him, then happened with Sarah, she leaned closer and closer until she fell through a flash of light and came tumbling down and down and down, growing smaller as she went.

"Aaaaarrrrggghhhhh" Thump. Sarah landed in the same soft spot of leaves that Jake had and looked around confused "Jake! Where ARE you?"

"It's ok, I'm right here"

Sarah spun round and saw Jake behind her, she ran to him and was about to hug him when she spotted Raven floating to the left of Jake, her mouth falling open in disbelief. For the first time in her life, she was actually speechless. Jake couldn't remember the last time Sarah had nothing to say and assumed rightly that it probably wouldn't last too long.

Sarah's eyes were wide in shock and her mouth was agape, she started to make some sounds but no words were coming out yet although she did keep looking from Jake to Raven and back again, then up at the tree trunk, trying to process it all.

It was Raven that broke the silence as she flittered towards Sarah slowly, a gentle smile on her face, holding out her hands in a welcome gesture.

"I'm Raven" Her voice was soft and kind "You must be Sarah, I didn't think you would be far behind" She added knowingly.

Sarah's mouth finally formed some words "You're a fairy" She breathed in complete awe.

"You knew we were coming?" Jake asked

"Of course Jake" Raven turned to look at him " You haven't forgotten your dream?"

"But that was a dream," Jake was astonished "Just a dream"

Raven laughed softly but not unkindly, she fluttered a little higher, rubbed her delicate hands together, a cloud of gold, glittery dust gathered around them

"Sometimes Jake, dreams are more real than we know" She delicately blew the gold dust towards them and they began to float in to the air until they were as high off the ground as Raven was. Jake and Sarah were amazed, their bodies suddenly lighter, the freedom they felt was unbelievable but Jake recognised it from his dream, Raven then came closer and whispered in his ear "Come with me" and they went.

They floated higher and flew with Raven guiding them deeper in to the forest, Jake saw and heard things he had never been able to before. Everything was so clear and big! The trees giant, the lines in the bark like huge crevices Jake could now get lost in but would usually run his fingers over them, the bird song so loud it filled his head but it didn't hurt. Noises usually hurt Jake, nature was different though, it soothed him and he soaked it up. He felt like he belonged right here, the woody scent of the forest filling his nostrils, warm air rushing past him as they glided slowly towards an enormous oak tree, they began to fly higher up and up and up until they were half way and in front of a large doorway. If Jake had been normal size it wouldn't have looked like a door way it would have looked like an oval shaped indent in the bark, but up close like this it was clearly a doorway with a stone hanging on a piece of rope for a door knocker. Raven didn't use the door knocker, she simply placed her hand on the door above the knocker and held it there for a moment. Her hand glowed gold and the door clicked open, she gestured for Jake and Sarah to come through with her other arm and a reassuring smile.

Nothing could prepare them for what they saw upon entering the fairies home. Their faces fell in amazement as they stared in wonder.

"I must be dreaming" Sarah breathed as she took it all in.

The fairies home was magnificent. Inside the oak tree there were hundreds of other fairies scattered about in various places, all busy in their own way working. Some sculpting figures out of wood, others whittling furniture, some spinning cotton in to rope, some carrying twigs and leaves to different parts of the tree which in itself was incredible. The tree appeared to be completely hollow and there were lots and lots of different levels with tunnels; rooms, little fairy dens, communal areas, cooking areas, spaces for tiny beds, all lit up in thousands of lights. The fairy den was busy and beautiful, colourful with natures gifts: things were held together with spider web that glimmered in the light, there were fairies making clothes, some cooking right at the bottom of the oak tree, the smell wafting up to invite everyone to join. But majestic of all was the illuminating light pulsing through the centre of the tree which started at the bottom, reaching right the way to the top. It was thick and had tiny veins of light coming off it reaching in to every little fairy room, connecting to everywhere, right at the top the light continued but Jake couldn't see where it went. The whole place was alive with magical hustle and bustle, normally the sort of noise Jake would despise, but here his ears weren't offended in any way, he revelled in it and could not wait to explore!

"This is unbelievable!" Sarah had finally found her voice "It's like a dream! Jake! Are we dreaming?"

Raven floated towards Sarah "We've been waiting for you two to arrive. Sometimes dreams and life can be one and the same and sometimes they can be quite different" Sarah didn't understand the riddle, neither did Jake but neither did he care. There was only one place he wanted to be right now and that was here.

"Come, lets meet everyone" Raven gestured for them to follow her down in to the heart of the oak tree

"My goodness Jake, we are FLYING"

"Floating actually Sarah"

Sarah rolled her eyes at Jake, "Now I know it's not a dream, talk about ruin a moment"

When their feet touched the ground it felt odd after being in the air so long. At the bottom of the tree two fairies regarded them with interest. They kind of skipped over shyly. They were both blonde and very slight, one was a little taller than the other but they looked very similar. The taller one stepped closer, she was wearing a light pink dress, her long blonde hair in two neat French plaits that reached her waist. She eyed them eagerly and when she smiled, the corners of her eyes crinkled and you could see she was kind and happy. Both Jake and Sarah liked her instantly. The other fairy stayed back a little, more shy than the first. She had the exact same shade of blonde hair but hers was worn in a high ponytail and she was wearing a yellow dress. She was interested too, but didn't come too close.

"I'm Ruby, this is my sister Jessica" The first fairy said excitedly "We're so pleased to meet you" The smile didn't leave her face and you couldn't help but smile back

"Hi I'm Sarah. This is Jake" Sarah had now found her feet and was as usual far more confident than Jake in speaking to other people and now... fairies! "Hi Jessica" Sarah continued

Jessica waved and smiled but stayed silent and a little reserved while she watched her new visitors intently.

"Jessica speaks through her hands in sign" Ruby explained and stepped back to stand with her sister "And I always translate" Ruby put her arm lovingly around her sister.

"Nice to meet you Jessica," Sarah said "This is my brother Jake, he doesn't always speak either and I kind of do that for him too. Although he doesn't use his hands, he just normally speaks when there is just the two of us or we're at home"

 Jessica smiled at Sarah and turned to Ruby to sign something, Ruby nodded and signed something back

"What did Jessica say?" Sarah asked

"She said friends?, so I said yes they are friends" Ruby explained

Jake waved awkwardly, Jessica waved back.

 Raven showed them the first floor, where they had their fairy gatherings and ate together, There was a large room past the cooking pot with sweet little wooden stumps and round backs , painstakingly carved by the fairies no doubt. The chairs were all the same except for one that sat at the head of the very long table. That chair was wider and taller than the rest and had a symbol on the back of it that Jake had never seen before, it was a leaf, but inside it the veins of the leaf created a heart shape, then a smaller heart shape inside that and another inside that so it looked like it was pulsing.

 In the large dining area, another fairy was busy sweeping the floor and repositioning the chairs. He was so quick at his work, almost haphazard. He skittered from one chair to the other then the other side of the room to something he had seen then back to his original spot. His energy was relentless and he was chatting to himself the whole time. Until he saw his new visitors.

"My goodness! My goodness! Human people! Can't be, can't be. You're far too small to be human. But you are exactly like them!" He rushed over, an excited smile on his face making his cheeks blush. His eyes wide and clear showing how blue they were.

"I'm Rowan" He grinned when he came over. Rowan was not shy at all, just so pleased to greet his new guests. Then it must have dawned on him as he sucked the air in dramatically in realisation

"You ARE human! You must have found the magic portal in the woods. Why, that is incredible no one has ever found it. It has been hidden for thousands of years and only to be used in fairy emergencies!" Rowans floppy mousey brown hair flitted about as much as he did. He darted about on both feet, one then the other, one then the other, one finger to his temple while he thought about it. "What was it like? Did it hurt?"

Raven stepped in then.

"Rowan, this is Jake and Sarah"

"Hi Jake, Hi Sarah!" Rowan held out his hand and shook it furiously with excitement "So good to meet you"

Rowans energy was infectious and they couldn't help grinning back at him. Sarah giggled, she really liked him. Rowan was a lot like her, so full of excitement and a little all over the place.

"Well, it didn't hurt going through it" She said answering his question at last "And luckily when I landed it was on some leaves so I was ok"

"Woah" Rowan said incredulously "You're so lucky!" Then looked at Jake for further explanation but Jake felt a little overwhelmed to speak so smiled instead. Sarah understood immediately and filled the silence

"It's really good to meet you too"

"Ok Rowan, I'll continue with the tour, see you later on" Raven said and gestured for them to leave as she waved to Rowan who went straight back to his work tidying, sweeping the floor and arranging the chairs.

"Where are we going next?" Sarah was fascinated, her earlier shock completely gone.

 They went in to what was the kitchen; there was a huge cauldron type pot cooking over a fire, its contents simmering gently and releasing the most welcoming smell. There were hundreds of wooden bowls stacked up neatly on the shelves carved out of the oak tree itself, saucepans hanging in a row on one wall, cups hanging on another by their handles, a big sink and lots of tea towels folded on another shelf. There was one long table here with a fairy busy chopping ingredients and adding them to the pot. She had her back to them and Jake noticed that she was older than the other fairies, slower. She had long white hair pulled back in a messy ponytail, strands falling across her forehead as she concentrated on her task. She wore thick rimmed glasses like big circles around her eyes which she had to keep pushing back up her nose because they kept slipping down. She had pale skin and wrinkles, her eyes twinkled with a mischief that denied her age, making her seem much younger than she was.

"Hello Raven, " She pushed her glasses back up on her face and peered over them at Jake and Sarah "Well, who do we have here?"

 Raven went closer in to the kitchen "Come on, don't be shy, come and meet Honor. Honor is our oldest fairy, we all rely on her for her wisdom, her patience and her cooking too" Raven smiled warmly at Honor who in turn dismissed the compliments with a shake of her hand and hovered over to Jake and Sarah.

"I really should walk when I can, to burn the extra calories. But if you've got wings then use them I say"

"I wish I had wings" Sarah confessed

"Oh they can get in the way sometimes" Honor pushed her glasses back up on her nose again "I've had to jump in the sink more than once when getting too close to my fire here" She winked

Jake liked this fairy, he felt calmer, easier. It surprised Sarah when he asked:

"What are you cooking? It smells delicious"

"Ohh, this is stew. But it's like stew you've never tasted as our ingredients don't exist in your world. This is my very special Oak side stew. I named it Oak side because we have an allotment outside of the tree where I pick all of our vegetables. I don't think I've found a fairy who doesn't like it. Maybe if you stay long enough you'll get to try some"

Honor didn't ask any questions, she just made them feel very welcome and got back to her cooking. When they left Jake was feeling happy but couldn't understand how this was all happening and looked at Raven who seemed to understand his unanswered questions.

"Honor is our Elder fairy, she looks after all of us, she seems to know just what to say and do and keeps us all well fed. Whatever the problem is Honor somehow makes it better. Each fairy has a purpose, a role that fits them perfectly. We are all very, very different and that helps our world to flourish the way it does. I know you have questions, but I'm not the fairy to answer them. I guide, that's my role. There is so much for you to see, but maybe we should go now where your questions can be answered."

Raven took Jake and Sarah to the middle of the Oak tree where the illuminating light pulsated from top to bottom, connecting to everything in silken strands running off it. This seemed to be the beating heart of the Oak tree, Jake could hear something coming from it.

"Wow" He murmured walking closer "What is that?"

Raven looked quizzical "What Jake?"

"That noise. It's like lots of different voices talking coming from here."

Now it was Ravens turn to be surprised "You can hear that?" She looked at Jake, a little taken aback "Interesting"

Raven then picked up one of the strands from the thick light and spoke to it softly "Were ready" Rubbing her hands together and creating another gold cloud of dust, she blew it over them. Sarah squealed with delight knowing she would soon fly again and they followed Raven upwards, up and up and up they went to the top of the tree where all strands of light met and then flittered off separately in to the floor, pulsating with their brightness and vibrating with words. This room was big but simple, but the most extraordinary thing was the fairy they saw immediately when coming up. She was sat amongst the strands of lights, her long white hair, the same colour and shade as the strands of light attached the them. No wait, it WAS them. This was all her hair that flowed down in to all rooms and all the way to the bottom of the Oak tree and it seemed she was listening to all the words that travelled up to her. She was expecting them and when she saw them her smile radiated warmth and love.

"Hello Raven, Hello Jake, Hello Sarah. Please do sit down, while I unhook my hair or I won't hear a word you are saying"

She then took out a large gold band and tied her hair with it at the base of her back and pulled slightly, her hair then came free of the strands of light which was now held in a gold hairband. She carefully tucked it around a hook making sure it was secure before she turned to face them again.

She was so graceful and delicate, yet she emanated a strength within her. Without being told you just knew she was the leader. She wore white; her dress simple like the other fairies but she wore the symbol on her dress that Jake had seen on the bigger chair; the leaf with the heart inside, it was sewed on in an icy blue colour, her eyes were the same blue and her pink lips curled in to a genuine smile as she came closer.

"I'm Madelaine" Her voice was light and clear "It's lovely to meet you Jake and Sarah, please do sit down"

They had been too busy watching her to even look around but as she gestured towards the wooden chairs behind them, they all walked over and took a seat, again these had the symbols on them Jake had noticed, and soft white cushions on each chair. She had stacks of books in various places around the room, some open, some with book marks in. There was a comfortable looking bed, next to it a large sculpture of a tortoise, it had been painted a deep brown colour. Her lights glowed steadily above their heads.

Raven did not sit down when Jake and Sarah did, instead she made her way to the entrance.

"I'll see you soon" and off she flew, her wings flittering prettily as she went.

Sarah who had been pretty quiet for a while, began chattering excitedly "This is amazing! I keep thinking it's a dream and that I'll wake up at any moment, but I don't think it is, is it?!"

Madelaine laughed openly in response to Sarah's excitement. "Ohhh, you remind me of Rowan, you met Rowan didn't you" It was a statement not a question.

Jake nodded and knew exactly what she meant, Sarah WAS like Rowan, both happy and excited and full of chatter. Even sitting down here, Sarah couldn't sit still, she was tapping her feet and wriggling around in her chair.

"And you know Sarah, sometimes dreams are more real than we think" Madelaine said with a wink "Although you are indeed very much awake"

"So, how come we're here?" Jake asked, surprising Sarah again. Normally Jake couldn't talk to people. But these weren't people, these were fairies and Jake somehow felt comfortable here, he felt natural. There seemed to be complete acceptance. It was a nice feeling and for once he could feel his confidence start to grow.

Madelaine regarded his question carefully as she too sat down.

"Well, as you can see we are all fairies and as fairies we all work hard. We are all very, very different. We embrace those differences and build on them to make them our strengths. We have lived in harmony for hundreds of years as a community and that is the reason it works. One of the most important jobs of a fairy is to help people, animals, and other fairies.

We can hear exceptionally well, quite like yourself Jake, but us fairies have fine tuned the ability to mask out the other "White" noise as we call it. White noise is all that other stuff going on that is very distracting and sometimes distressing so that we can hear only what we need to." Madelaine got up and walked over to her strands of her hair tied neatly on to the hook "Listening is one of the most important things we can do, to each other's needs, problems, hopes and fears. If someone feels listened to, they can work with a problem and overcome something. If a problem is big and you are listened to, it feels less big, more able to manage, above all it makes us feel good. My job is to listen. I listen to the fairies all day, I can hear them hard at work, helping others, some singing, some laughing, some crying with sadness some days, some with a problem they may need help with and I know about it and as soon as I do, I will help. I just have to listen, I know by their voice that travels up to me who It is and we start to work with it together because we are a unit and if the fairies are happy, supported and listened to we all work well together"

Sarah and Jake were listening to Madelaine intently, but Sarah had questions.

 "So how do you hear them through that? What is that?"

"This is our life source, it connects us. Through my hair. We are all connected, fairies check in when they are at their work space and I hear them. I can also hear other fairies through the same room if they have gone in to see someone. "

 Madelaine let the information sink in for a moment, then clasped her hands in front of her, bringing it to her chest and leaned in to it, like she wanted to hug them; a gesture they would soon learn is something she often did to send love and wishes to someone.

"I heard you Jake"

 Jake blinked, looked back at Sarah and then back at Madelaine.

"H-how?"

"Like I say, my hearing is exceptional, a little like yours and you heard us too didn't you. Not many people can. But you feel at one with nature, it really is your calm place. So of course.." Madelaine said with a smile, "We knew you were coming, you too Sarah"

"So, you heard us in the woods?"

"yes, but, before that. We have been hearing you for some time"

"Do you hear me?" Sarah asked

"Of course! You are on Jake's line of communication and as you two are so close..where one goes the other is to soon follow. So you see, I'm so glad to finally meet you. When we heard you, we knew you would find your way here"

"The tree trunk" Jake said "That's where I first heard it, tinkling like laughter and I saw colours but then it was gone"

Madelaine nodded, "Yes, that was us, well Raven. We knew you would need some time to process what you had seen so that's why you would never have found us that day. After your dream we opened the portal"

"You know about my dream?"

Madelaine smiled "Sometimes dreams carry important messages we won't accept in waking life and they are far more real than we know"

"Yeah, I've heard that a few times today" Jake said but he guessed she knew that already.

"Why would you let us in though?" Sarah asked "I mean, why us?"

"To help you" Madelaine answered "When we have a call, we listen"

For the rest of the time there, they were shown around the beautiful place, every nook and cranny leading to something new to find. The fairies were all different ages, shapes, sizes and characters. Sarah liked Rowan the best, she went to find him after their talk with the head fairy and he was showing her how to fly with the gold dust without being led, all you could hear in the room was shrieking and laughter as she crashed in to things and tried to avoid the walls. Jake sat quietly in the kitchen with Honor as she made him a mug of warm brew, it was what the fairies drank. It wasn't like tea or coffee, it tasted sort of like creamy mushroom soup and was delicious.

 The other fairies came and went, curious about their visitors but none stayed too long or asked questions, they seemed to know how shy Jake was and they all stood and waved, smiling, offering their name and then flitted back off to the job they were doing before.

 Honor just sat there quietly drinking her own brew and another fairy silently flew in, her little feet touching the ground quietly. She had an wide grin, wild dark brown, curly hair and a deep red colour dress on.

"Hi" She came over to meet Jake. Honor then busied herself at the sink cleaning the cups. "I'm Heather."

"I'm Jake"

"I know" She grinned again and sat down, flicking her mad hair out of her eyes "This must be strange for you! All these new experiences! I've got to tell you I couldn't wait to meet you.. but had to wait my turn. Wow you're just what I imagined."

She leaned forward, completely comfortable chatting to him, as if they had been friends for years " Tell me, how are you finding our home?"

 Jake felt his shyness ooze away as he chatted with Heather about the fairy way of life; how incredulous and amazed he was he was even here, how he loved the brew, about the food they ate, the jobs they all did. He asked her questions about her job. She was responsible for upkeep, she made sure everything looked nice, had fresh flowers and let the other fairies know who needed to if something wasn't working. Heather was warm and open, she wore her heart on her sleeve and was straight to the point. You didn't have to guess with her how she was feeling or what she meant, she spelt it out for you. Jake liked that a lot, he always found reading body language really tricky.

 Sarah came bursting in with Rowan, laughing and crashing about, they were so similar that both of them together made double the noise. Jake grinned, as much as he hated noise, he loved Sarah and it was great to see her like that.

 Raven hovered in behind them watching them and smiling. It was a nice sight, they were all relaxed and happy together, talking and laughing.

Honor busying herself by the sink as usual; putting on another brew. She didn't want to break it up but knew it was time to take them back.

Heather was the first to notice her.

"Ahhhh, already" She said nodding, but reluctant to say goodbye.

Jake and Sarah spun round "We have to go?"

"I'm afraid so, you've been here quite some time and although fairy time is stretched out much longer than human time, you will still be missed if you stay any longer"

"Oh my God! Mum! She will be wondering where we are!"

"It's ok Sarah" Raven said reassuring her "Fairy time is slower, much slower. But even so you've still been gone a while so It's sensible to go back now"

"Can we come back?" Sarah wanted to know, echoing Jakes thoughts

"Of course, we were all hoping you would want to"

Satisfied with that; Jake and Sarah said their goodbyes to Heather, Rowan and Honor and made their way to the centre of the Oak tree where Raven dusted them with a cloud of gold again and they lifted up slowly, the feeling make Jake grin, he was no longer scared; just happy. His friends below waved to him and he waved back, his sister by his side showing off her new moves Rowan had taught her and waving as well, it really was like a dream. Raven guided them to the entrance in the middle of the Oak tree, the door opening and sunlight spilling through. The sound of birds chirping filled the air and Raven closed the door behind them

"Let's go" Raven flew first and then hovered to turn and encourage them out of the ledge they were standing on. Sarah couldn't wait, she jumped with excitement and squealed with delight as she flew outside, Jake was far more nervous. It was one thing to be floating in the safety of the fairy den, but quite another to be the size of a lady bird and jumping off the middle of an Oak tree, it was a very long way to fall.

"Jake, you will be ok. You are not going to fall" Raven reassured him, holding out her hand. He tried to get his breathing under control and focus on Ravens eyes in front of him. She was very calming and he felt better almost straight away

"Come on Jake! This is incredible!" After Sarah's crash course lesson with Rowan, she was much more confident than before and threw out her arms, flying upwards, then down, all the while laughing and happy.

"I'm here Jake, you will not fall" Raven's gentle, reassuring face began to fill him with confidence, he felt himself relax and he slowly stepped off the edge of the ledge. He floated, he did not fall. In mid air, the lightness surrounded him and laughter bubbled up inside of him, finding its way out of his mouth, he looked at Raven, smiling. She smiled back in a protective, proud way.

"Now fly Jake" Jake tentatively flew forwards, when after realising he wasn't going down unless he chose to, his confidence built and he went higher, towards the branches, then lower towards the ground. This small he could see so much more he never noticed before. The mushrooms at the base of the Oak tree with so much detail, the tiny insects that were not tiny now to Jake, he could hear their scuttling noises, see the beauty of life emerging through every pore of the earths surface. It was amazing! He flew back upwards towards Sarah who was doing a loop the loop in the air and tried to copy her, Raven hovered by and laughed watching them.

"It's time to go" She reminded them and held out her arms to guide them forwards. Raven flew in front and kept checking behind her to make sure they were following, it seemed they reached the tree trunk far too quickly and Raven guided them on top of it this time.

"It's over here" She gestured but Jake and Sarah couldn't see anything at all.

"What is?" Sarah squinted

"The portal"

 As they landed on the tree trunk, Jake noticed a shimmering in the air, it reminded him of the fairy wings, he could see everything through it like a giant circle in front of him but it waved slowly.

"There" Jake pointed it out.

"I see it" A hint of sadness in her voice, Jake knew she was sad to go but that it was time.

"We will come back"

"When?" Sarah wanted to know

"As soon as we can"

"Bye Jake, bye Sarah. See you soon" Raven waved and Jake turned to Sarah "You first, I'll follow"

 Sarah stepped through, there was a flash of rainbow light and she fell out the other side, she rolled twice then POP was her usual size again. When Jake saw she was safely through, he turned to Raven and waved "Thank you", he stepped through then and the light surrounded him, he rolled, then the world around him wasn't so small anymore. When he stood up, he felt huge, like a giant! He was the size he had been before he had entered the portal, but after being the size of a ladybird, he now felt enormous, like 10 feet tall!

"Wow!" He said adjusting again

"I know, that was incredible!" Sarah exclaimed "I wish I could still fly!"

 Jake turned round and searched for Raven or a flicker from the portal but could see nothing this time. It was time to go home, he wondered what time it was! But definitely time for food; Jake was starving.

"Come on Jake, let's go home, get some lunch, tell Mu-" Sarah stopped dead in her tracks, even she realised without Jake saying anything that this wouldn't be something they could share

"We can't tell anybody about them can we" She said earnestly. "People wouldn't leave them alone, they would come over here all the time looking for them, their beautiful place would be ruined" Sarah, somebody who has never been able to keep a secret in her life due to complete excitement was determined not to speak a word of it to anybody and Jake could see that she wouldn't. She was as in awe of the fairies and their home as he was.

"No, " Jake agreed " We can't"

After agreeing to protect the fairies by not speaking about them, they made their way home. Both quiet and reflecting on their time in the tree. When they stepped through the kitchen door, they were surprised to see it was only almost lunchtime.

"Where have you two been?" Their mum came in then, carrying the hoover and two rubbish bags at once looking happy that the housework was finally done. "The woods again? Have a nice time?"

Jake and Sarah glanced at each other and smiled

"Yeah it was good, really quiet" Sarah said for them "What's for lunch?"

"Tomato soup and bread. Get the bowls out please dear"

 It was strange not telling Mum, they usually spoke about everything. But they told themselves it wasn't a lie exactly, just something not to be spoken about.

CHAPTER FOUR

School dragged by. Jake didn't like school anyway. He liked his lessons and most of his teachers; he loved learning new things but there was so much about school that he hated that he could never wait for it to be over. He was anxious about when he would be able to visit the woods again; it had already been two days but it had been pouring down with rain after school and mum always did dinner at 6 which didn't leave lots of time, and then there was homework as well. It looked like it was going to be Saturday before they would get to go again. The thought of three more days at school until he could go was stretching ahead of him like a promise, but he consoled himself with what he had to look forward to at the end.

Jake found school really difficult; the assembly's where so many people were crammed in to the one hall, all the kids talking. The steady hum of the chatter reverberated through his ears until he shook. Sometimes one of the nicer teachers would spot Jake and bring him out to wait in the hall where he could still hear, but others they left him there, they thought it would do him good to get used to it. Jake didn't think he would ever get used to it. The giant hum would last until the vice principal came along (Jake particularly did not like her) Miss Kerble. She had wild blonde hair that looked like it had never seen a brush stuck up in all directions on her head, big glasses that she pushed up on her nose but looked over the top of them so Jake never understood why she done that and she never listened to anybody. She would sweep in, in her long dresses and sandals with bangles rattling all the way up her arm and very strong smelling perfume. Jake always noticed her perfume, it was enough to choke you and then she would begin on addressing the school on whatever was important that week before handing over to the headmaster Mr Mumford. He was so tall with a long nose and a deep voice but Jake liked him, he seemed OK, although Jake never knew what was said and was always chastised later on because he hadn't listened but they never understood that he wasn't able to listen. He was pressing his thumbs in to his ears so hard to stop the hum that still remained and the echoes that bounced off the walls from Mrs Kerble's high pitched voice, concentrating so hard not to get agitated by the constant shuffling of other kids bums, prodding and poking by knees and shoes, scraping of chairs that he was literally shaking just trying to be in the room. Sometimes he didn't notice the tears streaming down his cheeks until someone laughed and then the whispers would start. If he was taken out, then everybody saw and It just made everything worse.

He didn't have friends at school, he didn't want those kind of friends anyway. The kids were mean, they called him names, pointed at him when he didn't understand PE, laughed when he dropped the ball. Jake had never been great at catching balls, he was a little clumsy. But he was great at keeping score and following rules, he was never asked to do that though.

The corridors between lessons were the worst! All kids at once being piled out in to the corridors out of one lesson to get to the next lesson on time and sat down meant lots of noise, shouting, pushing and shoving. It scared Jake; he would always try and keep out of the way. Crowds scared him, his breathing quickened and he would press himself against the wall, closing his eyes until it was more quiet then run to his lesson, making him late, all eyes on him as he scurried through the door and to his desk as quick as he could before the teacher could reprimand for lateness yet again.

In lessons, Jake felt calm, there was no talking allowed and he was able to learn but his incredible shyness meant he was unable to put his hand up to ask a question or even answer one when he was called upon. This meant even more attention drawn to him and more ammunition for the kids that teased and bullied him.

Breaktimes were awful, the 15 minute morning one, everyone ran out so fast and making so much noise it always forced him to the spot until everybody had left, then he would slowly make his way outside and find a quiet space, sometimes on the way he might see one of his nice teachers who would stop and speak to him, even though he didn't speak back, he was grateful for the effort they made. Mrs Pittman was especially nice, she seemed to understand him a little more than the rest of them and encouraged him to sit in her class room for five minutes gathering himself: she would chat about the weather, what they would be learning in the next lesson and never ever expected a response. When Jake was feeling a little better he would look up and smile, Mrs Pittman would then show him to the door, knowing he needed her to take the initiative in him leaving and he would go outside, or if he was lucky break time would be over and he would be able to get straight to the next lesson without joining the rush. Lunch times, Jake would venture on to the school field, go as far as he could and lean against the weeping willow tree, tucked away from everyone else and eat his sandwiches.

Jake loved to learn but he hated being in school. By the time he got home his ears were throbbing, his body tense and his throat ached with unshed tears. He would usually go straight to his room and lay there for a while trying to feel normal, sometimes this would take an hour, if it had been a hard day, sometimes two. Sometimes he would sob while his Mum held him, soothing him and talking gently to him. He would eventually feel better and it would be dinner time, then time for homework and shower, then bed and he would have to do it all again the following day.

Jake suffered terrible stomach aches, mum said it was because of his anxiety, he just knew it hurt and lately he had had blinding pain in his left eye, had thrown up and the pain in his head made him unable to stand, these were migraines mum said and usually came on when he was worrying too much about school and the activities they were planning: like school trips, sports days, school plays! Why did he have to take part?! Couldn't he just sit in his lessons and learn, wasn't that what school was meant to be about? The teachers felt it was good for him to get used to things, but it just made everything worse, the bus they had to travel on made him sick and he would end up having to sit with the teacher with his head between his knees and would shake when he saw the other vehicles on the road... being so high up highlighted his travel sickness and his fear of public transport, the kids were so loud as always and excited to be getting out of school, when the teachers yelled at them to be quiet, Jake was thankful but hated the yelling, it made him shake even more.

Most of the time mum would get him out of things, she was always talking to the school about Jake and ways to help him; they used words like provision, social understanding and sensory overload. All Jake really knew is that nothing ever changed, no one seemed to be listening. They would often tell mum that they offer him choices about whether to join in or not, but it was more like coercion and Jake knew they thought they were doing the right thing but for example Miss Weir would, in her lovely soft voice say to Jake "Hey Jake, why don't you just come to the dance class and stay on the side lines, you can them watch everyone else, see what they are doing and join in when you feel ready" As she was leading him to the hall with the thumping loud music and kids doing a complicated dance routine.

He envied those kids, that were unhurt by the noise and the hectic way that school was, the way they so easily made friends and laughed as they went between lessons, joining in in all activities, seemingly to sail through with no problems. He WANTED to be able to join in, but he couldn't. Nor could he say no, because he was unable to speak. The plug in his throat stopped him from saying a word and Miss Weir as usual mistook his silence as agreement and guided him in to the hall where the noise pierced his ear drums and he fell on the floor shaking and crying In front of the whole class. Miss Weir said she was proud of him for trying and he got bullied for the whole term over it.

Mum would say to him "Jake can you say no to the teachers when they want you to join in? They just think I'm being over protective but I really think if you could just try and say no to them it would really help"

Jake would shake his head, knowing his words wouldn't come. Sometimes at home, his words came out and they didn't make sense to him because he was upset, so if he did speak at school and that happened he would get bullied even more, plus most of the time he was trying his best not to cry, so speaking out loud was hard.

At home, Jake could be himself and he loved being at home. His room was his sanctuary, he soaked up his books with a thirst for knowledge and often impressed his mum with information he had learnt. His room was navy blue, grey and white. Everything was in order, everything made sense. His room was calm and quiet, he had his TV, Xbox and Nintendo switch, his own bathroom and his window looked out on to the fields leading to the woods; Jake loved his room. Sarah would burst in unannounced all the time with her continuous chatter about her day, she was like a ray of sunshine on a dark day. They were complete opposites, but they were best friends. Jake never minded when Sarah would come in and make a mess, she would mostly clean up before she left and she needed her big brother:

she looked up to him and he needed her just as much. Sarah was the only one Jake really could be himself around. She was the one who knew him the best.

Thursday afternoon was drama class and Jake had a terrible stomach ache all day knowing it was coming. He felt so physically sick he couldn't eat any lunch and by the time the bell had sounded the headache had begun as well.

All his class had lined up outside the drama hall and they were all excited because most of them loved drama: it was an opportunity to act silly or show off or for those that took it seriously to really act out. Jake had his back to the wall, trying to block out the noise of the line waiting to be let in when Charlie Marden pushed him, it was so unexpected he almost fell over.

"You gonna cry again Jake? Cry baby!" Charlie was one of his constant bullies, he wasn't in every class, but seemed to be there right at the worst moments ready to taunt him some more. He had dark brown hair, was quite short, a sneer on his face that never went away and mean dark eyes. Charlie had a following of about seven friends although Jake wouldn't call them friends, they just did whatever Charlie told them to do as he would turn on them just as easily. His mouth was ten times bigger than him and everybody stayed away from him if they could help it.

Jake pressed himself hard against the wall, hoping Charlie would leave him alone and the teacher would come along but she was late today.

"What's your problem Jake baby? Not learned to talk yet?" He crooned in a mocking voice, his face inches away from Jakes.

The line started to fall silent so they could hear what was happening with Charlies latest victim

"Don't ignore me Jake, its RUDE!" Charlie got closer still, scowling at Jake and he could feel his heart thumping in his chest

"CHARLIE MARDEN GET BACK IN LINE THIS INSTANT!" Miss Laindon had finally come around the corner and Jake breathed a sigh of relief. Charlie got back to his place but not before digging Jake in the ribs with his elbow and laughing to himself as he did so.

The class piled in quickly and Jake hung back not wanting to enter but not wanting to draw anymore attention to himself

"You ok Jake?" Miss Laindon asked him before he walked through.

Miss Laindon was nice, she seemed to like Jake, but she didn't listen either. She had light brown hair that was always tied back in a loose bun, tendrils of loose hair floated about her eyes and she blew it away absent mindedly as she talked to Jake.

Jake wasn't ok, his stomach was in knots, his head hurt and he wanted to cry. But he couldn't say anything so he kept quiet and put his head down.

"We're going to do something a little different today, we will work in threes; two children will do the acting and the third will pretend to be filming it so the third person does not have to speak if they don't want to." She was a kind teacher and Jake liked her, he wished he could open his mouth and say to her the hall bounced the kids voices off its walls like an acoustic nightmare for him, that he could barely understand what was going on as it all happened so quickly and he couldn't keep up, how he felt that everybody's eyes were on him, how his breathing would get faster and faster, how he hated even being here in that hall. But he couldn't form the words, the plug was back. He could barely look up right now, he stayed silent and Miss Laindon smiled gently at him "Come on, I'll put you in a nice group"

"Right everyone, quiet down! I'm putting you in groups of three. No Charlie, you're with Freya and David, You three together" She started pointing out sets of children "You three, you three" Miss Laindon pointed then at two of the nicest and quietest children; Sharon and Mathew, and Jake "And you three. We are working as teams, two of you will act out an interview. One of you is the interviewer, one will be interviewed. It can be about whatever you like and the third will "record" it" She used quotation marks in the air when she said the word record. Miss Laindon walked over to Jake's group "Jake will be filming your interview ok guys" And walked away so there was no discussion over their roles.

There was a lot of chat and quarrelling about how everyone would present theirs, the groups getting louder and louder, breaking off and larking about until Miss Laindon would tell them to quiet down and then they had 10 minutes of practice left before they had to perform to the whole class. Whole class. Jake couldn't focus, couldn't stop his head hurting, his stomach churned and he felt sick, every noise pierced his ears, he couldn't do it, couldn't do it. He could already hear Charlie's mean laughter ringing in his ears and didn't even realise he was leaving the room until he heard his nasty voice shouting after him.

"OI! Cry baby! Where you going?"

Miss Laindon found Jake curled up in a ball under a table in reception.

"I have explained to you before Miss Laindon that Jake feels very uncomfortable in drama and doesn't want to take part"

Jake could hear the conversation through the closed door as he sat outside in the hall. Miss Laindon had called her after she found him and was concerned about him.

"You see I do offer Jake plenty of opportunity to take part in other ways, I give him opportunities to say no and he voluntarily walks in to take part in the class"

"That's because he CAN'T say no!" Jakes mum was exasperated "And he's terrified of being told off. He speaks at home, all the time. It's school, it's overwhelming for him and certain lessons get too much, with the noise and chaos"

"My lessons aren't chaotic!" Miss Laindon sounded offended

"Not to you." She softened her tone "But everything is amplified for Jake and he tries his best to hold it in but then it becomes too much"

There was silence in the room for a while and Jake couldn't figure out what was going on.

"I do understand what you are saying, but it is a difficult one for me. My lessons are on his curriculum and unless he tells me otherwise I need to try and include him in creative ways in the class. He doesn't have to perform, he can do other things, but to be able to transfer him to another class I need Jake to let me know that, however he can"

"Did today not show you that already?!" Jakes Mum's voice was getting louder.

Miss Laindon just didn't understand how hard it was for Jake to communicate, and felt her classes would eventually help Jake communicate with kids in his class and his teachers by acting out real life scenarios. She cared about Jake, but wasn't getting it at all.

 On the way home, Jakes mum explained their conversation, although she hadn't needed to because Jake had heard it all. Sarah was in between them holding each of their hands "I'll go and tell her!" She said protectively and Jake appreciated it, he smiled warmly at her.

"I know I've said before Jake and I know it's hard. But Miss Laindon feels it needs to come from you. Is there anyway you can simply say no?"

 Jake stared at his feet. More than anything in the world he wanted to say no, he was scared to open his mouth in case his voice cracked, he said the wrong thing, upset anyone, so many reasons and usually the plug stopped him. Jake told no one about the plug. He didn't want people to think he was any stranger than they already did. Did other kids have a plug in their throat? He doubted it, but then his mind wandered to Jessica the fairy who didn't speak, and for a moment he felt a little happier remembering his time in the Oak tree, it seemed like ages ago, not days that they had been there.

"Jake" His mum stopped walking and looked at him "If you can, just shake your head, she will see it is coming from you and that may be enough. Just try ok?"

Jake nodded "Ok"

That evening Rebekah made pizza, chips and garlic bread, she pulled the sofa round in front of the TV and put a film on. The sound was on low and they sat and ate comfortably and quiet, squashed up together. Mum knew how to make him feel better and he went to bed feeling lighter but anxious about school the next day. At least it would be Friday and they would have two days off, Jake reminded himself they would go to the woods and that thought kept him going.

When Jake went to his room, he climbed in to bed and looked out the window towards the field leading to the woods, he longed for it to already be the weekend.

A warm wind blew through the open window and in blew a leaf, Jake was about to brush it back out again but something made him pick it up. He turned it over in his hands when he saw that on the leaf was the symbol of the head fairy in its veins. His heart leapt! Had she heard him? Did she know? Oh he wanted to go already, just one more day at school. Just one more day. Jake hugged the leaf to his chest and grinned. The day now forgotten, he laid down with the leaf in his hands and eventually fell asleep dreaming of woods and fairies and gold dust that made you fly, mushroom soup and the head fairy sitting in her room holding her hair and listening to all those around her, helping who she can and loving everyone with all their differences that made them unique. He slept with a smile on his face.

CHAPTER FIVE

Friday was uneventful thankfully and Jake didn't have Miss Laindon's class again until next week, what was even better was Charlie wasn't at school. Jake navigated the halls in his usual way and slunk in to lessons behind everyone else after the pushing and shoving was out of the way in front of him, and looked forward to his weekend. He was given homework but knew he would finish it tonight to get it out of the way.

Relief flooded through him as the bell sounded and everyone started packing their things away, scraping back their chairs and running out the door ready and eager to start their weekend too. Even the teacher looked relieved. Jake was the last out the door and one of the last out of school, wanting the madness to go ahead of him.

It was just a ten minute walk home from school and Jake would meet mum and Sarah there. Sarah was still in primary for the next two years but when she came to Jake's school she could join one of the after school clubs she had been wanting to go to; She always wanted to do activities she was so outgoing, mum could work a little longer too she had said.

As Jake turned the corner to the little shop he saw Charlie and his mum. Charlies mum was a really large woman, she had big blonde hair and a big mouth too. She was shouting at Charlie and swearing; Charlie was staring at the floor while his mum ranted at him, not caring how loud she was. Jake crossed the road to walk past, feeling very uncomfortable. He hated Charlie but instinctively he felt sorry for him all of a sudden

"What's the matter with you boy? Are you stupid or something?"

Charlie mumbled a response

"What?! Speak up! I can't hear you. Cat got your tongue?" This was a phrase Charlie used on Jake a lot

"I said no Mum"

"I'm telling you If I get any more calls from that school, boy.." She said menacingly.

Charlie was naughty in almost all his lessons... apart from Mr Goodwin's lessons. Nobody was naughty in them; you daren't do anything but breathe in that class (Jake liked his lessons) Jake assumed the school had called Charlies mum in over his behaviour again.

"Oh, pack it in cry baby" She growled at him. Another phrase Charlie used on Jake a lot.

Jake really felt sorry for him now, even though he had made Jake's life a misery, this was horrible to hear and then he heard it. SMACK. Jake turned just in time to see Charlie fall against the car they were standing next to and hold his face. Charlies mum walked round to the drivers side and got in. She yelled "Get in or I'm going without you and stop crying or I really will give you something to cry about!"

Jake watched as Charlies tears fell down his face silently, his head bent and got in the car. His mum revved the engine and drove away but for a split second; Charlie looked up and locked eyes with him. Jakes heart jumped in to his throat, he felt he had seen something Charlie definitely wouldn't have wanted him to see. He stood there for a moment, unsure of what to do. What could he do? If he told his mum, she tells the school, they contact his mum then Jake knew Charlie would know it came from him. He felt sure of one thing; Charlie would be very mad at Jake for telling everyone.

Jake walked home slower than ever, the excitement of the weekend ahead of him suddenly gone and all he could think about was Charlie.

CHAPTER SIX

"Wow you guys are up early today! Looks like you've got plans, where are you off to?" Jake and Sarah wasted no time Saturday morning, they were up, dressed and had their breakfast by 8 o clock. Jakes mum walked in the kitchen bleary eyed after having a bit of a lay in.

"We want to go on a walk and have a picnic mum, might be out for ages is that ok?"

"Where are you going to go?" She asked, switching on the kettle for her morning coffee. She always said she couldn't function without it.

"The field for a bit then have a picnic in the woods." Jake hated lying, but Sarah found it much easier, although they weren't technically lying were they?

"Ok, as long as you stay together and Jake take your phone in case of emergencies"

"It's in my pocket"

"Good. Now let's pack you guys a picnic" She busied herself making them cheese sandwiches and crisps, threw in two apples and a chocolate each. It made her so happy to see them so close, they needed each other and she would be able to get on with some housework with them out for a bit too.

"Make sure you're back for about half one, ok?" She handed the picnic bag to Jake to carry "You've still got all your homework to do"

"Yeah" It had been Jakes plan to finish all his homework last night but after what he had seen he couldn't focus on it at all.

"Come on then!" Sarah tugged Jakes hand, the excitement in her eyes shining bright. She looked like she might burst. "Let's go"

"Have a great time guys" Mum leant in for a hug with them both "Love you sooo much" She kissed them each in turn. "Go, on, have fun."

 Off they went, both of them feeling excited and happy, half running and half skipping through the fields. Sarah running ahead, putting out her arms in a stretch, then spinning madly around and around and around. "I'm so gonna try this in the air!" She shrieked. Jake laughed at her as she fell in the grass. "Well try not to do THAT!" He said pulling her up again.

"I wonder if they know we're coming" Sarah asked Jake

"I think they know" He nodded, remembering the head fairy sitting in her room listening to all that goes on. She had said she heard him too; and that leaf on Thursday night.. It was a message from her he just knew it.

 The sun was shining, there were barely any clouds in the sky, it looked like it was promising to be a beautiful sunny day. Jake felt happy for the first time all week and they ran the last part of the field to enter the woods. It was much cooler in there, the sun not able to get through the thick branches full of green leaves, shielding the forest like a secret blanket. They were quieter when walking in, as if it would be disrespectful to be too loud somehow. Wasting no time in finding the tree stump; Jake and Sarah were soon standing in front of it and Jake heard the tinkling sound, saw a flutter of colour and knew the portal would be open for them.

"Do you want to go first? Jake offered, He really wanted to see it from this side too.

"Yes! I sure do" Sarah stepped forward in front of the half tree stump until her foot was almost inside it and leaned forward slowly, she got to the angle where it looked like she might fall over and then she was gone in a flash of white light but Jake could hear her joyous laughter on the other side of the portal as she landed softly on the leaves at the bottom. He heard more tinkling and guessed it was Raven, he couldn't wait any longer and smiling he leaned in to the portal and fell down and down and down until he was next to Sarah on the leaves.

 Raven smiled at them

"Morning"

"Morning "They both said standing up and brushing off the leaves.

"What did you bring?" Raven had seen the picnic basket.

"Sandwiches, crisps.. You know the essentials, we want to stay longer this time but Mum said we have to be back by 1:30 today. Is there a way of knowing when that will be?"

"Of course. I will make sure you are here human time at 12.30 so you will be back by 1. But you needn't bring food. Honor has been cooking all morning in preparation for your arrival. Everyone is very excited, it's going to be quite a feast!"

Sarah grinned, loving the sound of a feast and sitting round the big fairy table with everybody

"Well, we can share our sandwiches then and add them to the feast" Jake offered.

"Perfect" Raven looked like a statue, sitting perfectly still on the mushroom in front of them, they heard a slow movement; a rustling in the leaves, then from behind Raven a huge black spider bigger than them came slowly creeping out from behind a rock.

Sarah's mouth opened in horror; she hated spiders anyway but this one could and probably would eat her! It was right next to Raven. Jake had lost the ability to speak and warn her but Raven didn't flinch. She then turned and smiled at the spider after seeing their faces.

"Hello May"

"Hello Raven" The spider responded.

Jake and Sarah were amazed. A talking spider! But then they were the size of ladybirds that had just gone through a portal to meet the fairies.

The spider (May's) voice was slow and deliberate, she was in no rush at all it seemed, that was surprising, usually spiders were quick.

"Madelaine would like some more silk thread please May" Raven stood up at last " She has a bag of dried mushrooms all ready for when you want them"

"Wonnnderfull" May said. "I'll get straight on it"

"This is Jake and Sarah, our guests at the Oak tree"

May looked directly at them and her huge eyes all eight of them seemed to know exactly what they were thinking

"Don't be scared" She said slowly and softly. She had a slight metallic sound to her voice "I don't eat humans. Or fairies. Just bugs" She scuttled to the side and before she disappeared again she added "And of course Honors delicious dried mushrooms"

Then she was gone, Jake and Sarah daren't move, Raven walked over to them.

"Please don't be scared of May, she is a great friend of ours and helps us out with the silk we need to make things and we in turn give her mushrooms that Honor dries in a special way.. just the way May likes them. We don't see her often, she has many children to look after, but she comes when she can and if we need her we know she will be there"

"I thought spiders were fast" Sarah wondered aloud

Raven smiled again "When they need to be they are, but May is almost 6 which is quite old for a spider so she tends to take it easy these days. Are you ready?"

They were both so engrossed in May the talking spider that they had forgotten about the golden dust. Raven was now rubbing her hands together forming a cloud and when it was big enough she blew it towards them. Sarah laughed in excitement and threw her arms up in the air, going up instantly. Jake was more reserved; he tentatively looked up, his feet leaving the ground, he grinned too now, feeling more confident with it and straightened his back looking where he wanted to go making him go higher and higher. He wasn't afraid this time at all, happiness rolled over him like butterflies in his belly and they followed Raven to the Oak tree; noticing the birds and insects on their way. It was all so big and he could have flown all day, the lightness washing all his weeks worth of worries away. The earthy smell of the woods filling his nose and making him happy. Sarah literally looped around in circles laughing and shrieking.

 "Look at me Jake!" As she tried to do it backwards "I was born to do this!"

 Jake laughed out loud as he watched her and Raven watched on with love in her eyes. Their work was just beginning but was already working. The children's lives had been difficult so far. There was a lot of love in their lives but there had also been pain, past pain and pain that continued on for Jake in different ways. The fairies were there to help. And help they would.

 They made their way to the huge Oak tree, flying up to the entrance; Jake noticed more and more the symbols of Madelaine the head fairy where he hadn't seen it before. It was etched on the door and the base of the tree.

 When they entered and the door closed behind them, the sound and activity of the fairies filled his ears and eyes and he grinned. The smell of cooking was strong, smells that Jake didn't recognise but smelt mouth wateringly good. The activity was a low hum of fairies busy about their work, apart from Rowan who must have spotted them immediately

"Hi!" He came over straight away "Oh I have missed you!" He grabbed Sarah's hands and they flew round and round in circles laughing. You couldn't help but smile seeing them

Heather was next to spot them " Hello, wow this week was so slow, I'm so glad you're here" She flew over to Jake, welcoming him with a big smile and not hugging him, Jake didn't like hugs unless it was Sarah or his Mum and even then not all the time; Heather seemed to know that about him and kept a distance.

"What have you got there?" Heather pointed to the picnic bag Jake carried.

"We brought a lunch this time so we could stay longer" Jake explained, feeling less self conscious now Heather was here, she made him feel at ease. She was chatty but not in a pushy way and seemed to know when he needed to be quiet.

"Wow, you were prepared! But you needn't have worried. Honor has been in the kitchen since early this morning making all kinds of mushroom dishes for us, bread, special tea, she's pulling anyone in

that walks by to wash up as she goes along"
Heather laughed.." She does love a feast"

Jake felt touched "Sounds amazing. She didn't
have to go to so much bother, but really we can't
wait. We will put our picnic on the table for
everyone to share too"

Sarah and Rowan had already disappeared
somewhere, to organise the dining table chairs
probably, Rowan was doing that the last time they
were here.

"What job do you have today?" Jake asked
Heather

"Flowers" She answered "Arranging the wild
flowers for the hall"

"Can I help?" Jake asked

"Sure! That would be great!"

They made their way to Heather's room which
was next to the flower room where there were
piles and piles of pretty wild flowers all around.
Blue bells, honey suckle, daisies, buttercups and
some that Jake didn't know the names of.

"Here, we take two of these, one of these and
two of these. Or maybe three of these" Heather

examined her own creation and added two more different flowers until it looked perfect "There. Just play around with it until it looks good. You have creative licence! " She pulled a piece of the string that was hanging with another stack of them from the wall and expertly wrapped it round forming a bow.

"This is cow's parsley" She explained picking up the white flowers on long stems, Jake had seen this before but hadn't known the name. "It smells so lovely and goes in almost all my flower displays, it sets it off just right. That's it.. You're a natural!"

Heather went through all the flowers and told Jake the names that he didn't know; forget me nots, cowslip, dogs rose and goats beard. They worked on the bouquets of flowers until there were a pile of them ready for the hall.

Heather and Jake made their way to the big hall carrying piles of flower bouquets each. Heather knew just how to place them so the hall looked fresh and inviting; they smelt sweet and light. The big table was long and Jake paid more attention to Madelaine's chair as he approached it, outlining the symbol with his finger, Heather noticed him doing this.

"That's our symbol. The symbol of connection"
She fluttered over to where Jake was and
explained further "The leaf represents life and
growth, the veins within represent the heart of
everything and that we are all connected, not only
to each other but to each animal, insect and
plant"

"Is it everywhere?" Jake asked, thinking back to
Thursday evening when he was alone in his room
and the leaf came in through his window like a
message.

"It Is where It Is needed to be" Heather watched
Jake carefully "Have you seen it somewhere
else?"

Jake nodded, "Thursday night, a leaf came
through the window with the symbol. I wondered
if it had blown in by accident."

Heather smiled warmly

"No Jake, that was no accident. Madelaine would
have been reaching out to you for whatever
reason." She fluttered over to the strand of light
that encircled the room which Jake now knew was
Madelaine's hair and their way of communicating.
She reached around and held a strand of her own
hair to it, immediately it fused together with a

glow of light. Quiet for several seconds, Heather stood still, then she gently nodded and detached both strands of hair.

"Ok. Time to see Madelaine" She held out her hand to gesture Jake forward with her and he felt a little hesitant. Knowing Madelaine heard everything made him feel embarrassed; she knew how he had been feeling. Then he felt comforted knowing she reached out to him when he felt so low. By the time they had flown to the top of the Oak tree, Jake was confused and a little uncertain, but just one look at Madelaine's face as she waited patiently for them, melted away his concerns as she looked up with only warmth and kindness in her eyes. She was so delicate, sitting there surrounded by strands of hair, listening to the thoughts of all the fairies and connecting with others that needed help and guidance. Gracefully she stood up, carefully detached her hair, pulling a band around the other strands and hooking it up on the floor so she could move away from it.

"Jake" her soft voice welcomed him in "So good to see you again" She gestured towards her chairs "Please. Sit down"

Heather left without a word, just put her hand up in a wave and flittered downwards, back to her work.

Madelaine sat opposite Jake, her expression serene. She looked in to Jakes eyes and leaned forward to take his hand

"I heard you Jake. On Thursday I heard you, I felt the pain and sadness you felt"

Jake looked towards his feet, feeling embarrassed, but then felt Madelaine's light touch as she ever so gently cupped his chin in her tiny hand.

"Don't look down. Always look up. I want to help you, and I can if you will allow me to"

Tears began to fall down Jakes cheeks as he told her things he had never told anyone; how he was afraid of the dark, how he couldn't speak to people, why school was such a nightmare for him and that he got teased every day. The way things built up over the day and he cried at school or tried to hide somewhere, making kids pick on him even more. The way teachers didn't understand him and he could never ever find his voice, the voice that the teachers were so desperate to hear. He even told her about the plug in his throat. Jake talked for a long time and Madelaine listened, he felt she already knew most of this, he didn't know how, but he had a feeling about that and when he finally stopped talking he was amazed that he not only had spoken for a long time; something he rarely did, but that he felt better.

"I know it's hard, I feel your pain Jake. I want you to know you are stronger than you realise and one day you will speak out. Your plug only has the power you give it, you can pull it out and you will, and once you begin to pull it out you will find things you find difficult will become less so, over time. "

Madelaine sat back "You speak here, tell me why is that?"

Jake didn't know how to answer for a second but then it came to him, it was obvious.

"Because I feel like I'm home"

Aside from being at home with his Mum and Sarah; being surrounded by nature, listening to the different bird songs, among the stillness of the outside, the earthy smell, grass, the flowers. The beauty of being in the woods, finding new things grow, trees changing with the seasons. It was his favourite place to be, one where he felt connected to the earth, grounded and happy. As far away from the polluted place that was school and hurt his heart and head day after day like a growing infection.

Jake didn't say any of this but he felt it and Madelaine nodded, she had heard him.

"I understand" She stood up and walked over to a large set of drawers next to a bookcase in her simple room. The wooden drawers were beautifully carved and had the symbol on the front of each of them. She went to the second drawer, pulling out a small glass bottle.

"This is for you" She brought the bottle over and placed it in Jake's hand.

"Open it."

Jake opened it and without needing to bring it over to his nose to smell the contents, the earthy smell of the woods after a downpour of rain with the subtle hint of flowers blowing in the breeze filled his senses. He looked up in amazement.

"When you need to be reminded of where you feel safe and happy, open this and remember you have a voice and only you can use it. Even a simple word is a start Jake, it will be the stepping stone for change"

"Thank you" Jake was touched by this beautiful gift and put it in his pocket straight away.

"You're very welcome. Now, I believe that there is a feast to attend."

Madelaine smiled and stood up, she held out her hand to Jake who took it. He felt lighter than he had in years, after talking how he felt about things, he felt happier, far less troubled and for this moment as he flew down the huge Oak tree next to Madelaine the head fairy who had given him this incredible gift, he felt happiness surround him like a bubble.

97

CHAPTER SEVEN

The feast had been incredible, every fairy had worked so hard at creating an amazing experience. The long, beautifully carved table was adorned with large bowls of food. Food that Jake and Sarah had never seen before; lots of it was to do with mushrooms which they were quick to realise were the fairies main source of food, but they learnt that there were many kinds; kinds that grew under the ground which people never saw.. although there were also poisonous mushrooms that could be deadly so only the most experienced mushroom pickers had that special job; those were Kate and Roy, they looked so alike they could be brother and sister; both had mousey brown hair with freckles splashed across their faces, their eyes crinkled when they smiled (which was a lot!) and they both wore green. Their one difference was that Kates hair was so long she had to plait it and then wrap the huge plait in a big bun and Roy's hair was short and fluffy, sticking out around his ears.

There was special tea that sat in big jugs around the table with every place having a wooden goblet; there were berries of every kind drenched in honey, nuts chopped up in to manageable pieces (It took several fairies to carry nuts as they grew bigger than them but these weren't nuts Jake had seen before and when he asked about them he was told they were called nibs; this was because they grew at the tops of the bushes they planted, they made milk from them as well. There was bread, mushroom soup, mushroom patties, onion soup, caramalised onions, salad leaves, so many things it was like a rainbow of food, it all looked so inviting and delicious Jake and Sarah could not wait.

Sarah had her place next to Jake and Rowan at the other side; they were fast friends now and chattered away constantly, laughing and poking each other. Rowan was always teaching Sarah about fairy ways, different flying techniques, she was fascinated and Sarah in turn shared with Rowan what she did at school and how their way of life was, Rowan was equally fascinated and between them they talked easily while helping themselves to the vast array of food surrounding them.

Jake, next to Sarah and Heather found himself opposite Jessica and Ruby. He had liked both of them when he first met them and smiled and waved at Jessica who waved back shyly. Jessica signed something to Ruby and Ruby asked Jake "Jessica says how do you like the feast?"

"It's amazing, I've never seen so much food!"

At that point, Madelaine tapped her wooden goblet on to the side of the table, it was a small sound but every fairy and person fell quiet immediately. She then pulled her hair around and pulled one strand down to the table, connecting it to something underneath, it wasn't until then that Jake noticed there was connectors at each space and every fairy in turn did the same, even those with shorter hair seemed to be able to do so; as they ran their hand through their hair, one long strand would fall down so they were able to connect to the table, with each connection the table gradually lit up in a series of lights travelling from their eating space to around the plates and bowls and finally up to a pole situated in the middle of the table with hundreds of individual strands that Jake had not seen before and now it glowed steadily with the beautiful light from the fairies all connected. Jake watched as they all closed their eyes as if in prayer for a moment and then the ceiling began to glow in the pattern of the symbol just like on Madelaine's chair... the symbol of connection. It was magnificent. Jake felt so privileged to be here and had to pinch himself to make sure he wasn't dreaming.

The fairies slowly opened their eyes and removed their hair from the connectors under the table but the lights still glowed strong and raised their goblets.

"To being as one" They all said together and resumed their feast and conversations that were happening beforehand.

"What just happened?" Jake asked Heather. Sarah seemed unfazed by it at all, but he had guessed correctly that Rowan had told her all about it before the feast had begun so she had known what to expect, after all they literally never stopped talking!

"Feasts are quite special to us, we only have a few a year to celebrate certain events and when we do all come together like this, it is important that we all connect and feel each other's gratitude and love for the work we bring to the tree and to ourselves. We appreciate each other and it's our way of coming together and connecting. As everything is connected. From the earth that grows the mushrooms that we enjoy now, to the wood that we use and carve out our furniture and the spiders that give us the silk for our material; we put back as much as we take and we all work together as one with different skills and abilities"

Jake smiled and was warmed by Heather's words. They really were special, he loved their way of life and how they looked after one another.

"What is the reason for the feast today?" Jake wanted to know.

"Well you two of course! " Heather grinned. "No human has ever been in our home before"

The fairies stuck to their word of getting Jake and Sarah home for 1 pm, reminding them when it was close to the time and to say their goodbyes. Raven guided them to the opening of the Oak tree after the feast, both of them feeling full and happy. As soon as the door was opened, Sarah whooped in delight and flew circles around them while Jake more serenely flew towards the tree stump alongside Raven.

"Can I go first?" Sarah wanted to know as she was already making her way to be the first through the portal.

"Sure" Jake smiled and watched her jump through it this time, rolling twice before POP back to normal size, she laid on the floor giggling and waiting for Jake.

He looked back at Raven who was waiting patiently for Jake to go through.

"Thank you" He wasn't exactly sure what for... for guiding them, showing them this wonderful place hidden by the magic of nature, being patient, all of it.

"You're welcome" She softly "Remember your voice Jake"

Jake remembered the glass bottle in his pocket and hoped it would survive going through the portal. He stepped through carefully and landed next to Sarah POP. Immediately feeling for it in his pocket, Jake was relieved it had gone through intact.

He helped Sarah to her feet, both smiling and feeling tired after all the food, flying and fun they had had with the fairies.

"We are so lucky" Sarah looked up at her big brother with a happy smile. No concerns on her lovely young face, Jake hoped it would always be that way.

"Yeah we really are" He put his arm around her "Right it's time we got back. I've got homework to do and you promised Mum you would clean your room"

Sarah deflated immediately, groaning out loud.

"Man Jake! You sure know how to put a downer on things"

Jake laughed " Your room is a disgrace though"

"Well we can't all be neat freaks like you can we"

They argued light heartedly all the way home, not speaking of the fairies but holding their special memories tightly in their own minds.

CHAPTER EIGHT

Sunday had passed too quickly. They had visited their grandparents; Rebekah's side. It was rare they got to see their Dads side. Rebekah made the effort to keep in touch with visits around birthdays and Christmas but it seemed to be one sided and they had less and less to say to each other. Their Nan would look at Jake and walk in to the kitchen with tears in her eyes, reminded of her son at that age, so cruelly taken away before he got to see his children grow up. Rebekah would hold in her frustration and try to keep things light, after all this was about the kids she always said when she was talking to her friend on the phone, why couldn't she hold it together for an afternoon and make it a happy time.

They loved seeing their Nan and Grandad. They would visit every fortnight and stay for a few hours. Grandad always made them laugh, Nan would keep giving them sweets despite Rebekah's groans about too much sugar and Rebekah would sit with her coffee talking to Grandad on the side of his good ear.

"Get the doll's house bits out Len" Nan ordered from the kitchen "Sarah wants them"

Grandad dutifully went to the shed, retrieving the toys for Sarah. She loved playing with the doll's house, It had been Nans for years and years. She used to make all the little food herself with clay, bought other pieces in charity shops and over the years had grown in to a child's dream dolls house, it sat in the corner of the living room, waiting for their fortnightly visit. It was the one time Sarah would sit quietly and concentrate for a while as she arranged it all just the way she liked it.

"It's a shame you don't keep your room that tidy" Mum Joked.

"My room is tidy." Sarah tried defending herself "I cleaned it yesterday"

"I think your tidy and my tidy are a little different darling" She nudged her with her feet and smiled.

Jake was sat at the kitchen table with his Nan working out a crossword puzzle, Mum and Grandad were discussing the cost of shopping these days and how so many things had gone up in price, talk turned to bills and grandad asked Rebekah if she was managing.

"We're fine. Really Dad, don't worry"

Len nodded, knowing his daughter was proud but he was in a position to help if she needed to or would let him.

"Well, if you need anything…"

"Thanks, I know" She went to take her cup out to the kitchen. It was a lovely house, spacious and clean. Len and Mary were both retired now but they had worked hard and been sensible. Mary followed her in to the kitchen lowering her voice.

"How is school?" She asked quietly, nodding her head in the direction of Jake.

Rebekah shook her head "Not good, some days are better than others but they just don't get it. They push him all the time to do the things he finds so hard and it sets him back each time. Sometimes I think maybe another school would be better but then he would have to start again and you know how hard he finds change. They just don't listen to me or him" She added "He may not be talking out loud but his actions are speaking volumes"

Mary nodded, she looked sympathetic and concerned for Jake but there was nothing new to say. They had had this conversation many times before.

"I just want him to be happy" Rebekah's eyes filled with tears thinking of the last time Jake had struggled in drama, ending up hiding under the table.

Mary hugged Rebekah, "He IS happy at home, you've made a beautiful loving home for them kids and you've done it by yourself Beck, just keep doing what you're doing. Maybe another school is the way, what does Jake want?"

"He doesn't like to talk about it, it upsets him so he clams up. He tries not to talk about any of it" Rebekah wiped her eyes "He will cry for hours some nights" She whispered "I just don't know what to do"

It was quiet in the big kitchen for several moments while Rebekah got hold of her emotions, she didn't like being upset in front of the children.

Jake could hear them talking, he could always hear them talking so he walked out in the garden, he didn't want to hear anymore. Besides, he knew his mum was getting upset, she loved him so much and hated to see him hurting at school.

Jake spent a little time in the garden, watching the ladybirds crawling over long grass, how tiny they were, how tiny they had been. He smiled then, remembering. He lost himself in the beautiful flowers around the edges of the garden. Nan was great at gardening; she knew just what to plant to look good and what stayed nice all year round, complimented by pretty flowers popping up everywhere in the summer. He was so immersed in the colourful flowers he hadn't noticed his mum coming behind him.

"They're so lovely aren't they" Rebekah put her arms around Jakes shoulders, pulling him closer for a hug "I wish I had Nan's green fingers"

"Why would you want green fingers?!" Jake asked incredulously

Rebekah laughed softly, but not unkindly "Oh Jake, I do love you so, so much" Planting a kiss on his cheek and hugging him a little tighter

"I love you too Mum"

They stood there for a while, the warm sun on their faces, listening to the birds squabbling in the trees nearby, smells of the flowers all around them and Rebekah knew they would be ok. Somehow.

113

CHAPTER NINE

Monday morning Sarah burst in to Jakes room as usual throwing herself on his bed, she was holding Betty, still in pajamas, her hair all knotty and sleep still stuck to her eyes.

"Morning" She yawned "Can't believe we have to wait a whole week to go back to the forest" She said glumly.

"I know." Jake was thinking the same thing. A whole week of school to get through first. He sat up "What time is it?"

"6.30. I wonder what they do at this time of the morning?"

"I don't know. But I bet Honor is making tea, the whole place smelling of cooked mushrooms, maybe the lights slowly lighting up" Jake thought aloud.

"Yeah" Sarah agreed. "I wonder if it is ever in complete darkness there. I'll ask Rowan next time"

"I can't imagine that" Said Jake. "I have an idea there is always light there"

"Me too. I'm still going to ask Rowan" Sarah decided.

"Morning you two! You're up early." Rebekah came in and found a spot on Jakes bed, she laid down with them both, having a big cuddle and deciding what was for breakfast before going to switch the kettle on for her coffee. "Can't function without it " She always said.

"Ok," Sarah jumped up "I'm getting ready, I'm starving. And I have mastered the cartwheel so I can show that show off Nancy that she isn't the only one that can do it. She's so mean to people too, never lets them play unless they can do what she says. Not that I want to play with her now, I have better friends but I want to cartwheel right past her group WHILE sticking my tongue out" Sarah was off and already thinking about the next part of her day leaving Jake to think about his and Charlie came to mind. He wondered if he would be in school again.

Breakfast was hash browns and beans, Rebekah loved cooking them a warm meal before all going out for the day. The table was littered with homework, Sarah's dolls, until she decided which one was joining her that day, lunch boxes, orange juice and of course Rebekah's coffee. They chatted easily while preparing for their day then Jake would walk to school. Sarah's school was in the opposite direction so Rebekah took her in the car but Jake didn't like being too early so liked to walk, making sure he got there just on time right as the bell went and held back behind the crowds of children going through the gates; laughing, pushing, talking about their weekend, calling out to one another.

This was Jakes first year in seniors, his third term and he honestly didn't know if he would ever get used to it. It was so different to primary where the teachers knew him and let him do different things when he was finding something difficult, it was also so much bigger! So many kids! So many class rooms, it was confusing. They did different lessons, some Jake liked but it was the madness that went with it that he couldn't cope with and Charlie who was making his life miserable whenever he bumped in to him. He didn't think he would ever make a friend but all he really wanted to do was get through the day without too much attention being brought to him.

Double maths was first, everybody was groaning about it but Jake didn't mind; he found the problems a challenge and enjoyed solving them, usually getting them right. This week is was converting fractions in to decimals and once he followed the pattern right, he found it easy, this made the lesson pass quickly, before he knew it, breaktime was here announcing itself by the shrill bell throughout the school. Jake instinctively put his hands over his ears and stayed in his seat until everyone had left, then slowly gathered up his books.

 "Good work today Jake" Miss Withers said to him as he left. Jake smiled and nodded, pleased he had done well.

 He made his way through the long corridor, there was still 10 minutes left. He could go in the toilets but usually groups of kids hung around in there so he kept walking. The long corridor would soon end and he would be outside. There were three separate buildings to Jakes school and three demountable buildings, two for science and one for music. The building he was in now was like a large L shape. His next lesson would be Science, in the demountable round the back. Jake didn't want to go round there yet, kids would usually hang around in groups outside where their next lesson would be; some kids were ok they just ignored Jake, but some teased him, especially if they were bored at breaktimes. He stood where he was for a few minutes, looking at his watch five, minutes left. Maybe he would just stay here.

"Hello Jake" Mrs Pittman came walking through the corridor at that moment, coming the other way. She was carrying three large bags, stuffed to the brim with books and papers. It looked heavy "How are you doing?" She made a quick assessment of his situation and realised he was counting down the minutes until break was over.

"Staying inside out of the rain. Very sensible indeed"

Jake felt himself begin to flush, he wanted to say something, but didn't know what.

"I tell you what, you wouldn't mind helping me with these bags to room 32 would you? They are awfully heavy"

Jake nodded and gave an awkward smile, picking up two of her three bags, he really was happy to help and followed her to room 32.

"Just over there please Jake that would be lovely"

Jake put the bags down, feeling awkward again, not sure what to do next. Two minutes left until the bell now.

"You know, I've been meaning to ask; I was speaking to Mr Geoffrey's who runs the library and we were thinking of starting a break time club for people who would like to read quietly at break times and you did come to mind. Is this something you would be interested in Jake?"

YES! He would, so very much! It would be so nice to have somewhere quiet to go and he did love to read!

Jake opened his mouth. It felt dry and strange, he tried nodding but Mrs Pittman was busy looking through her papers now.

She must have taken his silence for refusal because she said "Well if you do change your mind, let me know, you know where to find me" She smiled widely at Jake now

"Thank you again Jake, I'm sure you have a lesson to go to?"

Jake was still nodding but for the wrong reasons. He was so angry with himself! He wanted to say yes, that's all he had to say and his tortuous break times would be over, he would be able to sit in solace and do what he loved, read!

Jake started to walk towards the door then realised he had the glass bottle Madelaine had given him in his front pocket, he quickly pulled it out, taking off the lid. Instantly the sweet earthy smell of the forest filled his senses and his pulse returned to normal, he felt calmer and much more at ease.

"Yes" Jake croaked without even thinking about it. The sound came out dry, like someone who hadn't had a drink in a long time and quiet but it was definitely there.

Mrs Pittman looked up in surprise and delight. At first she was taken aback and didn't respond then she realised how much that had taken for Jake and quickly took the lead again.

"Wonderful. I will arrange it and let you know when it will start." She walked over to Jake, putting her hand on his shoulder. Her kind eyes smiling at him "Well done" She actually desperately wanted to hug the boy but that would have been unprofessional.

The bell sounded then, break time was over. Jake took his school bag and attempted to get out of the corridor as soon as he could before the doors burst open.

He could barely believe it! He said yes! He spoke!

School passed uneventfully that week until Thursday afternoon. He hadn't seen Charlie all week, rightly assuming he was still suspended for something or other. His mind kept going back to the afternoon he had seen Charlies Mum hit him. He couldn't get it out of his mind. Mrs Pittman hadn't gotten back to him either so he hoped she was still organising it and would let him know when she could.

It was drama and Jake was dreading it. The last drama class he had fled the room and hid under a table. Jake grew red just thinking about it. But standing here in the line waiting for the teacher with the noise building, the pushing and shoving, the worry of what he might be expected to do gave way to a familiar panic growing in the pit of his stomach. Jake rubbed the tip of the glass bottle wondering how this could help him here, he couldn't get it out now there were too many people. Miss Laindon wanted to hear it from him that he felt uncomfortable in his class. His heart started beating loudly in his ears, drowning out the children's chatter all around him. Quick deliberate footsteps came tapping on the floor.

Jake knew that was the teacher, she always wore high heels.

He closed his eyes now and tried to calm his breathing; instead imagining the smell of the woods, picturing the strong Oak tree. Jake wanted to be as strong as the Oak tree, as proud. Stood tall with deep roots in to the ground, the strongest wind in the world would not be able to topple it.

Jake had not noticed the class had already gone through, he did not know Miss Laindon was talking until she touched his arm. Jake opened his eyes and saw her smiling at him.

"Afternoon Jake" her smile widened "Joining us today?"

Jakes legs felt strong, like no one could push him over, just like the Oak tree. Slowly he shook his head.

Miss Laindon was quiet. Jake had never "said" no before. It felt like a whole minute passed by until she spoke again, her face showing how disappointed she felt.

"Ok" She resignedly accepted this, took a deep breath in, then smiled, crooking her neck to the side. Jake was worried she might be angry at him but instead picked up his hand with both of hers and looked him in the eyes.

"Let's see what we can do for you instead then"

Jakes heart leapt! He could cry with relief and happiness, having to mentally shake himself before he tried to move his legs that were standing so firm he worried they would betray him and he would be stuck outside the drama hall forever.

Miss Laindon threw open the doors to the hall, shouting instructions for the class to practise emotional responses in pairs, then turned to face Jake. She smiled "Come with me" She said. Her words took him back to his dream; Miss Laindon was no fairy but she certainly looked better in Jakes mind now.

They went to the office behind reception where there was a small room with a stack of papers haphazardly strewn on a table, and a soft chair. There was nothing else in the room, the window was open slightly, giving way to a soft warm breeze and the smell of freshly cut grass.

"As you know we will be doing a school play at the end of the year so I will be auditioning people for the roles" Jake actually had no clue this was happening, probably because in assemblies he was either taken out or was pushing his hands to his ears so hard he could only hear his own pulse.

"So here, I have fifteen different scripts for the play, I asked the junior receptionist to photocopy them all for me which she did, however she dropped them all in the playground, they got blown everywhere so are all mixed up. The pages are numbered and I need you to organise them for me, can you do that?"

Jake nodded enthusiastically, he was great at organising. This was perfect for him.

"Wonderful! Thank you!" Miss Laindon clapped theatrically "Well I will get back to class before bedlam ensues"

Jake had no idea what she meant by that but he was so happy. He hadn't spoke, but he had found a way, she had heard him and listened. He was being helpful which he loved, so immediately got to work sorting the scripts in to piles along the floor, smoothing them out and ordering the pages, determined to do a good job. Jake enjoyed sorting through the papers; he found a system that worked and had just finished the last one when Miss Laindon came through the door with a stapler.

"Oh my! You've done it!" She exclaimed "That's marvellous Jake, thank you ever so much"

Jake smiled, he stood up.

"Well the bell has gone now, you can go. Did you not hear it?"

Jake had heard it but didn't want to leave until he had finished the job.

"Well, have a lovely evening Jake. See you next week"

Jake left school feeling buoyant for the first time since he had started there. He couldn't wait to tell his Mum and Sarah.

CHAPTER TEN

Finally Saturday came. It had actually been a good week for Jake and for the first time since he had started secondary school he was feeling more positive about it and less sick. If only Mrs Pittman would approach him about the lunch time club, that would help so much at break times when he was trying to be anywhere else but around crowds of noisy kids, all relieved to have some rest bite from their learning day.

Mum had made a celebratory dinner when he had told her what had happened with drama, she was so proud of him for making a stand and letting his feelings known. Jake thought she looked more relieved than he did! She made a buffet style dinner of cheese and tomato pizza with wedges, salad, corn on the cob covered in butter and garlic bread. They snuggled together and watched a film of Jakes choice, he had had a great day and was feeling happy.

Saturday morning Jake was up early and dressed, making a picnic for him and Sarah. They hadn't discussed it but they both knew where they were going.

"Morning guys" Rebekah looked half asleep when she came in to the kitchen, automatically switching on the kettle, searching for her favourite aquamarine cup her best friend bought for her birthday; It had such a big crack running down from the rim to the base that every morning Jake worried her cup would crack and spill the entire contents over her but she continued to use it because it was her favourite.

"Wow, you two just never lay in do you" She smiled while spooning coffee granules in to her cup. "Where is it you are off to today? And is that a picnic I spy?"

"Sure is" Sarah was busy filling the bag with fruit and filling up bottles of water "We are going for a wood walk again Mum, it's so pretty there and Jake loves the quiet. I'm taking some dolls to play with, is that ok?" She went over for a hug and smiled up at her mum, she had such a cheeky but loveable grin.

"It's ok. But you stick together" She looked at Sarah "Do what your brother says and don't leave your dolls there" Then looked at Jake "And be back by 1:30"

"Sure" Jake zipped up the picnic bag "What are you going to do Mum?"

"Housework" She answered sipping her coffee "and probably pop to the shops. Do you have your phone?"

"Yes and it's charged"

Rebekah, saw it wasn't yet 8 o clock

"Are you going already?!"

"It's so nice there first thing in the morning mum" It wasn't a lie, it really was. The birds sang sweetly, you could see the squirrels scooting up the trees and around on the ground in search of food, the morning dew made the spiders webs look magical. Jake just loved the woods.

"Ok, you've had breakfast?"

Jake and Sarah were pulling on their trainers now

"Yep" Sarah answered "and bowls are in the dishwasher."

"Ok, well looks like I've got the morning to myself then. Have a great time guys and remember be back by 1:30. Love you"

"Love you too mum" They both kissed Rebekah and hugged her before hurrying out the back door and heading to the field. Sarah had Betty her favourite doll and Daisy the next favourite. She wanted to show Rowan, she felt sure he would like it and they could make them fly with fairy dust. Jake didn't bring anything, he just wanted to be there again, maybe help out in the kitchen, see what Heather was up to today and he would like to say hi to Jessica the fairy who didn't speak. He wanted to see Madelaine again and just sit with her, she was so peaceful and understanding it made him feel at home.

They walked purposefully across the green, buttercups and daisies popping up everywhere; Sarah would stop occasionally to pick some, then begin skipping.

Sharing this with Sarah made them closer than they were before, like an unspoken bond between them. They rarely discussed the fairies at home, both their experiences at the Oak tree completely different ones but equally magical and memorable to them both, special to them for different reasons.

 Upon entering the woods, shade fell over them immediately, changing the view completely from bright sunny blue sky to huge trees reaching out tall and wide all around them, covering their area like a blanket of protection, little rays of sunlight would penetrate thinner branches casting a light on some areas making it look even more enchanted than they now knew it was. Mushrooms were popping up everywhere; Jake paid much more attention to them now wondering if any of those were in the delicious meals they ate, but remembered the warning that some could be dangerous so the job was only for the mushroom pickers. He wondered if they were out now picking mushrooms and how did they pick them when they were so much bigger than them, a thousand questions filled his head. He breathed in the woodland smell, closed his eyes and let his mind and body relax. The breeze carried along sweet smell of honey suckle growing not far away in the field, birds tweeted, the leaves scratched along the ground. Sarah broke his reverie by whooping as she jumped from a fallen log holding both dolls in to the air

"Whoooo" Falling on to the ground, rolling over, she jumped back up again completely unfazed.

"You can't fly yet Sarah" Jake laughed "Come on" Jake wanted to spend more time exploring, seeing what had changed in their place but he didn't want to waste any time going to the Oak tree either, he knew they would be waiting for them.

Making their way over to the tree stump, Jake saw the familiar flickering of colour above it and knew the portal was open for them, gesturing for Sarah to go first, he watched her lean forward closing her eyes, grinning. Complete trust that she would not be hurt when she fell through and then she disappeared but Jake could still faintly hear her excited joyful screams on the other side.

Jake next, smiling in anticipation he leaned in to the tree stump until he fell, putting his hands out in front of him, waiting for the soft landing of the leaves, he could already hear Sarah talking excitedly to Raven who sat serenely on the same mushroom as before waiting patiently for her guests to arrive.

"Good morning" Her soft voice spoke to Jake as he stood up.

"Good morning "Jake replied.

"That reminds me," Sarah began "Do fairies sleep? Like we do?"

"We do" Raven answered. "But we don't need quite as much sleep, maybe 2 to 3 fairy hours every afternoon"

"You don't sleep at night?" Sarah was intrigued.

"No, that's the best time to pick mushrooms and forage berries; when most of the woodland creatures are sleeping"

"Wow" Sarah was impressed. She was quite for a moment "But how do you see anything?"

"Our hair lights the way" Raven stood up, amused by Sarah's questions. She began to rub her hands together, fairy dust forming in a cloud before them

"Your hair lights up!?" Sarah was incredulous "Like at the feast? "

Raven cupped her hands out in front of her, a suitable pile of fairy dust gathered in her hands now, then blew gently, the contents covering Jake and Sarah.

"Yes" She answered as she watched them both start to float "Just like that"

"Cool" Sarah held her hands up in to the air with both dolls and flew upwards "I can't wait to ask Rowan about it"

Jake floated gently next to Raven, thinking about the image it had given him

"That must look amazing" he said

She nodded, "It is pretty special." She agreed "We all have our different jobs and work in teams"

"What do you collect?" Jake wanted to know

"I don't collect, I guide the teams to their locations, then fly between each team to make sure all is well. When collecting is finished I guide them back to the Oak tree"

"The same as you guide us"

"Exactly"

"Does Heather collect flowers? " Jake wondered aloud.

"She does. Rowan helps with the berries, you have to be quick with that one, thorns can really get in the way so he is perfect for the job. You've met our mushroom pickers haven't you. Jessica collects the honey, she has a special connection with the bees which none of us have, they allow her in and she fills jars of honey. " Raven flew upwards quickly to bring Sarah down, she had gone a little too far

"Let's stay in the shade of the trees Sarah, I wouldn't want a bird picking you up for breakfast now"

That was enough to make Jake not want to hang around anymore and they hurried to the Oak tree. Raven could sense his unease "We are safe in the shade Jake"

They flew past the rings of mushrooms Sarah had been studying, under sweeping branches and around trees. It was invigorating feeling the warm summer air flowing through his t shirt, hearing Sarah's happy cries, the familiar smell of the forest, the sweetness of the flowers surrounding it made Jake feel happy.

The big Oak tree ahead of them now; flying up to it and finding the door, Jake was excited to go through and see everyone. Once it was opened, Sarah was first inside; Rowan was already waiting for her. They whooped like old friends that hadn't seen each other in years, hugging and flying round in the air in a spin, then before Jake could say anything else they had gone. Jake could faintly hear Sarah's voice fading away as they flew to the bottom of the tree. He smiled to himself and wasn't a bit nervous this time.

Heather had come to greet him straight away.

"Hi!" She came over but didn't hug him like Rowan hugged Sarah, Jake liked his space and Heather sensed that. Heather wore a big smile and had lavender in her hair. Somehow she had managed to plait it with the lavender in it. It looked lovely and Jake told her so.

"Thank you. I had some left over after making my flower arrangements so seemed a shame to waste it." She flittered over holding a glass bottle to show Jake "I started making perfume for Ruby. What do you think?" She opened the bottle, holding it towards him. The subtle scent of sweet roses tickled his nose.

"Wow, that's lovely, you made that? How?"

"Why thank you" Heather seemed very pleased. "I hope Ruby likes it too. I used yellow rose, strawberries and water" She smiled looking pleased with herself, "I was on my way to give it to her now would you like to come?"

"Sure, let's go"

They found Ruby with Jessica, they were always together. Ruby had been busy tidying their room. It had two beds side by side; the strands of light from the middle of the tree came in to the room to light it and was pulsing gently creating a soft light. Jessica was sitting on the floor, her long blonde hair in a pony tail today. She had in front of her piles of glass jars, maybe thirty or so of them, she was wiping each jar carefully with a cloth and checking the inside then placing them neatly in rows. Each time she placed one down she would rock back and forth a few times focusing on the jar and hum before picking up the next one.

Ruby's eyes lit up when she saw Jake and Heather enter their room, immediately stopping what she was doing to greet them.

"Hello!"

"Hi Ruby, It's finally ready for you"

"Wonderful! Thank you Heather!" She smiled openly, reaching out for her perfume, after inhaling the scent her smile grew wider "Oh It's just what I wanted. You really are sooo clever" Ruby took the bottle to Jessica to smell. Jake was intrigued how they communicated, they had such a strong bond. Jessica sat quiet for a while, then bunched her right hand, wiggled her fingers up and down in front of her nose, she then bunched her hand again in front of her chin then opened her fingers to outstretched moving it backwards in an arch. Ruby made her hand a small fist and made a knocking motion downwards and repeated Jessica's last hand sign.

"Jessica says it smells beautiful and I agree" Ruby said coming back to them

"That's marvellous, I'm so happy you both like it."

"Oh we do!" Ruby turned to Jake now "It's good to see you again" She had seen Jake watching the exchange between her and her sister "Have you ever used sign Jake?"

Jake shook his head.

"Well some are quite easy. This one is hello" She simply waved her hand "This is yes" Ruby showed Jake the moving down fist she had done before "And this is no" Ruby Made her hand flat then moved it in a straight line. Jake copied her hand movements as she done them

"That's it!" She smiled and Jessica looked up at him then, Jake waved at her, she waved back then continued wiping the glass jars, putting them in rows again.

"Communication doesn't have to be about words" Ruby looked fondly at her sister.

Jake and Heather waved them goodbye as they flew slowly out of their room

"Where are we going now?" Jake wanted to know

"I thought you may like some brew. Let's go see Honor"

Jake and Heather went to the bottom of the Oak tree, he was fascinated with every turn, every bump, every little den lighting up in to a room. He barely noticed the gentle hum of the fairies wings anymore: In fact, there were no noises here that scared him at all, he felt entirely safe.

Honor was busy at the table chopping ingredients, she had a large wooden mug in front of her filled to the brim with brew, behind her was a large saucepan bubbling away, smelling inviting to them both.

"Brew's ready" She said As if she was expecting them; pushing her glasses back up after slipping too far down her nose, she looked up "Grab a mug each and you can help"

Heather flew to a shelf high above the sink; it held hundreds of mugs just like Honor's , the shelf itself did not look strong enough to hold all those mugs; it was thin and looked very old. Honor saw him looking and must have read his thoughts as she followed his eyes

"Ahh" She nodded "Things may seem weak but they are stronger than we think they are" She sipped her brew, continued to chop mushrooms and gestured for Jake to sit down. Heather had ladled large measures of brew in to the mugs and joined them.

Jake picked up his mug, the warm grey liquid not looking as appetising as it tasted. It warmed him through, making him feel happy and satisfied.

They sat around the table talking about Heathers perfume she had made for Jessica and Ruby, how lovely Honor's brew was and what she was going to be making for lunch that day. It was cosy and comfortable. Heather straightened up suddenly, then pulled her hair round to connect to the light pulsing gently on the table.. Madelaine's hair.

"I have to go Jake" She said after a moment's silence: pulling her hair back around in to place again "Madelaine needs a little help with something"

"Jake will be fine with me dear" Honor carried on chopping the last of the mushrooms, pushed them to the side and scooped them in to an enormous silver pot. It certainly was enough to feed all the fairies. She then pulled out a big bag bulging at the sides; hauling it on to the table, lots of shiny red, apple shaped items tumbled out.

"What are they?" Jake had never seen them before. He picked one up, examining it "Looks like an apple" Although it's skin was much more like a pepper.

"These are tops" Honor took an extra knife from her drawer, bringing it over for Jake "They grow underground, like much of our food does. Here", she passed him the knife.

"I'll show you how to cut them and you can have a taste"

The pops tasted sweet and savoury all at once, it was very different to what Jake was used to.

Honor laughed at the look on his face and Jake blushed "Trust me, once they are in with the mushrooms, onions and broth you will love it" When she smiled her whole face crinkled with it, but her eyes were clear and bright. Jake wondered how old she was, but knew it would be rude to ask, instead he thought of a different question.

"How long has this Oak tree been here?"

"Oh now there's a question!" Honor sat back in her chair and pondered the answer for a few moments. She screwed her face up in thought.

"You know I can't remember exactly, but for a very, very long time. Almost as old as me"

"You're older than the tree?" Jake couldn't help asking.

Honor thought for a moment

"Actually no, the tree must be older. Oak trees can take around 75 years to mature. But I come from a different place. It was so long ago.." She shook her head trying to remember " We had to give up our home, had lived in it for hundreds of

years, well our fairies did.. not me personally "
She smiled, the smile faded as she started to
remember " It was a beautiful place I'm told and I
have very few memories of it. I was just a baby
when I came here. The fairy trees were run
differently then too, they were more separate."
Honor took a mouthful of her brew and continued
chopping the pops

 "It was never said we were divided but we were.
Certain fairies lived together, there was no
mixing. You may have noticed that we are all very
different here, well that was the case in our old
woods but the differences were separated. We all
lived by doing everything we needed to do on our
own. Life was hard" Honor nodded " We worked
from morning until night, gathering water, food,
supplies, making our own items.. everything. But
we didn't know a different way. We all noticed
that certain fairies had better ways of doing
things, like a natural ability for it if you like.
However we never really helped each other, we
just carried on in our own dens which were much
smaller then and tried to do everything by
ourselves. Then one day everything changed. Our
woods were torn down" Honor looked sad and
lost in thought as she recalled the story to Jake "I

believe it was for something else to be built, but we lost many fairies. The ground rumbled like the end of the world and for many of us that's just what it was. My parents saved me, I was one of the lucky ones, a few out of each den escaped before the trees fell and we flew away."

"That's awful!" Jake couldn't believe what he heard

"Yes, it is." Honor agreed "together in tragedy the fairies found a new place to live. Here. I was a baby and my parents have long since passed in to the earth. As the days passed after the great tragedy, many fairies came and found us and we began to live together as one. We now recognise each other's qualities and strengths and we work together for the good of us all, we are all connected you see. Although we didn't see it before, it took something bad to happen before we realised how to live better and now we do. Once we were all together in one tree we wondered how we had ever survived differently. Then something magical happened"

"What?"

"Madelaine" Honor sipped her brew and looked at Jake "The more we communicated, the lighter the tree became and we didn't know why, each room grew a strand of light, it grew longer and reached in to every corner, lighting all the darkness. It grew upwards reaching everywhere, it pulsed like a heart. We didn't know what it was, we just knew it was important. We followed it and found Madelaine at the top: She has shown us how to be together, how to use our strengths and to embrace our differences to connect us all and we have lived a better life since"

"So how old are you?" Jake just had to ask

Honor laughed "Well I certainly am quite old. I am 202."

"Woah" Jake was impressed "Really! How old do fairies live?"

"I'm not sure, as my parents passed younger than I am. But I don't feel old. I'm just a lot slower than I used to be." She smiled "More brew?"

"Yes please" Jake held out his mug for it to be refilled as he listened to the elder fairy. She was fascinating.

"Fairies aren't born the way you were Jake" Honor began again "They are created by connection, a connection that has changed since we have lived together in this tree for over 200 years now. There were many empty rooms when we first arrived and slowly light found it's way in to those rooms, soon after that, there would be a cocoon, after many days the cocoon would break open and a fairy would appear. All rooms are now filled and the tree is alive with fairies and light. We have recovered from the dark days. Sometimes to move forwards, a drastic change is needed and that change can often hurt us." The old fairy paused in reflection for a moment "But we are stronger than we know and we can achieve more than we think"

The last few ingredients were plopped in to the pan as Honor stood up. The pan was enormous and needed to be moved on to the fire on the floor.

"Will you help me with this my dear?"

Jake didn't think he could possibly lift the pan it was so big but he couldn't refuse and he couldn't let Honor lift it by herself. They each took a side and lifted, Jake surprised at how he was able to manage it. They floated over to the steady fire, gently setting it down on the metal rack over the top.

"There. Shan't take too long now"

"Honor?" Jake had been wanting to ask a question

"Yes Dear"

"H-how old is Madelaine?" He asked.

"Nobody knows. I don't think even she does. Some fairies think she was born by the creation of connection when we arrived at the tree. All we do know is that together we are stronger and much, much happier. Talking of Madelaine I think she may be expecting you today. Do you need Raven to guide you or can you remember the way?"

"I think I can remember"

"Ok then" Honor began to rub her hands together, a cloud of gold dust emerging in her hands as she did so "Just in case you need a boost" She blew it over Jake; He instantly felt even lighter and floated upwards.

"Wait until you're in the hall or you'll bang your head on my ceiling!" The old fairy laughed grabbing his hand pulling him down again. "See you at lunch Jake"

Jake waved goodbye, making his way out of the room. Looking up the tree was enormous, rows and rows of rooms lit up by the pulsing light. Lit up by Madelaine. He suddenly became quite nervous, Raven was usually there, maybe he was wrong to think he could do it alone. Hesitating, Jake walked more in to the centre of the hollow tree, trying to focus, he looked up again, it was so high.. what if his fairy dust wore off, what if he fell? What if..

"Hey Jake!" Sarah's loud voice seemed to come from nowhere, she was grinning and flying towards him. He laughed: it seemed Sarah was born to do this, she was not afraid of anything.

"Where are you going?" She had Rowan by her side as she usually did while they were here

"To see Madelaine"

"Ohhhh really? Can we come too? "

"Sure, let's go"

Jake, Sarah and Rowan all moved up at once, Sarah chatted nonstop about the hundreds of fairy rooms they passed on the way up and flew in circles as she went upwards, Rowan loved everything she did and copied her. Jake noticed that they each had one of Sarah's dolls, it made him smile to himself when he saw them making the dolls fly in loops as well.

When they finally reached the top, Madelaine was sitting amongst her hair, eyes closed and concentrating: She stayed that way for a long moment before carefully removing the hair from her own and tying in the band she kept by the hook on the floor next to her. Facing them she smiled and outstretched her arms.

"Welcome" Her voice was like soft music.

Madelaine sat down in one of the chairs, gesturing for the others to join her.

"How are you all? Oh that's beautiful Sarah, what is it?"

Sarah picked up her doll proudly "This is my doll Betty, Rowan has Daisy"

Madelaine looked intrigued "May I?" offering her hand out to hold the doll.

"Yes!" Sarah sat up straight holding out Betty, pleased to be able to show the head fairy something special.

Madelaine traced her fingers along the stitching, turning it over, smiling at its face.

"Betty is very beautiful" She declared, handing the doll back. So how have you been?"

"Great! Me and Rowan have been playing all morning, but he has been showing me cool stuff too: Like how he can make his hair glow for night time gathering, and who makes your material for the clothes. I can't remember her name though.." Sarah screwed her name up in frustration as the name escaped her.

"Ahh, Tara. Yes she is extremely talented at making our clothes and we certainly keep her busy"

Jake hadn't met Tara yet, there were so many fairies busy about their work that he had yet to meet and so many jobs they were each so good at, it was fascinating to learn about. He loved helping Honor in the kitchen and talking to Heather who included him in her tasks. Jessica intrigued him with the way she communicated and was understood by her sister.

"Rowan, I wonder if you might introduce Sarah to Jacob, he is our carpenter" Madelaine suggested, seeing Rowan beginning to get unsettled for sitting still too long.

"Ooh you will love Jacob, it's so clever what he does!" Rowan instantly grabbed Sarah's hand "He makes all our chairs, carves designs on them, makes the tables, our mugs as well!"

"Wow ok!"

Without even goodbye, they were off, heading downwards somewhere, laughing and looking forward to meeting Jacob. Sarah had always been so busy flitting from one thing to another, Jake couldn't keep up! Rowan was just the same, it made Jake laugh.

"They are certainly alike aren't they" Madelaine observed watching them go.

"Yeah, they are."

Jake looked back at Madelaine and felt she knew already but wanted to tell her how the bottle of scent had helped him this week.

"Thank you" He began

Madelaine sat and waited for Jake to continue

"This week a teacher of mine offered me a chance to join a lunch time club so I can sit in the library away from everything and I couldn't speak. I was so frightened if I didn't say anything she would think I wasn't interested and she wasn't looking at me so didn't see me nod. She had so many papers to sort out" Jake recalled "But I had the bottle with me, I smelt it and it calmed me down. I could smell the forest and the beating in my ears went away and I spoke to her. I said yes!" Jake smiled "I've not been able to do that since I was younger in my old school"

"Oh Jake that's marvellous! I am so proud of you." Madelaine leaned forwards and took his hands in to her own: Her touch was light and warm. "You did that. You. Nobody else. The scent reminded you of who you are, a way to focus yourself if you like, but it was you that spoke" She sat back and smiled

"Something else happened too" Jake told Madelaine how he was able to shake his head when it was drama lesson, one of his worst lessons, his teacher listening to him and offering him an alternative activity to do which she ended up being so pleased with what he did. Madelaine smiled widely.

"We are all so different and sometimes it takes time to find our strengths, but when we do and others see them, they can grow. I see YOU growing Jake"

Jake couldn't put his finger on why the image of Charlie came in to his mind at that moment and what he had seen with his mum, but he tried to shake it off, it left him feeling something he didn't understand.

Madelaine sensed his change "Is there something else Jake? Something you need to talk about?"

Jake didn't know how to put that in to words just yet. He found himself just shaking his head. Madelaine simply nodded.

"Ok" She tilted her head back, smelling the air "Looks like it's lunch time. Are you ready?"

They flew together all the way down the tree, following the light. The dinner hall was already full of hungry fairies taking their seats, chatting and bustling around. Heather had saved a seat for Jake and waved him over as soon as he came in. Every place had a wooden bowl and spoon that Jake guessed had been carved by Jacob. Once he had taken his seat and Madelaine hers, four fairies came in to the dinner hall carrying the enormous pan Honor had been working on earlier, she came behind with a ladle. They began with Madelaine, stopping at her place with Honor carefully ladling the soup in to her bowl then worked their way around the table until every place had a full bowl. Once everyone had their food then they began to eat. It was so tasty and filling: he enjoyed every mouthful. Sarah was even quiet while she ate. The meal passed too quickly and Jake knew it would be time to go home afterwards.

Sure enough, Raven appeared when the bowls were being cleared away but Jake was ready to go. He had had an incredible time as he always did and he was ready to go and be alone with his thoughts. They said their goodbyes, flying off towards the door after another cloud of gold fairy dust to get them on their way. This time Jake didn't hesitate after the door was open, he was as quick as Sarah flying through the air, knowing he was not going to fall, he even kept up with her and could hear Raven laughing as she lagged behind.

"Thank you Raven" They both said when landing near the tree stump, ready to go through the portal. Jake could see it easily now at a glance, before he had to really look and now he wondered why it took him so long.

"You're welcome, see you soon and take care"

Sarah first, then Jake followed: through the portal they went. Jake sat up, looked over at Sarah and saw she was simply laying there with her dolls looking up at the sky through the branches of the trees above them smiling.. content.

"We're so lucky" She finally said.

"Yes we are" Jake agreed. He got up, pulled Sarah to his feet and put his arm around her "Time to go home"

Rebekah was waiting for them at the kitchen table.

"I missed you guys! Did you have fun?" She embraced them both together, kissing them in turn.

"We did" Jake told her "Missed you too though Mum"

"Shall we watch a film now? All my house work is done and the shopping too"

Sarah jumped up and down "Yes please, can we make popcorn too?"

Rebekah laughed "Of course".

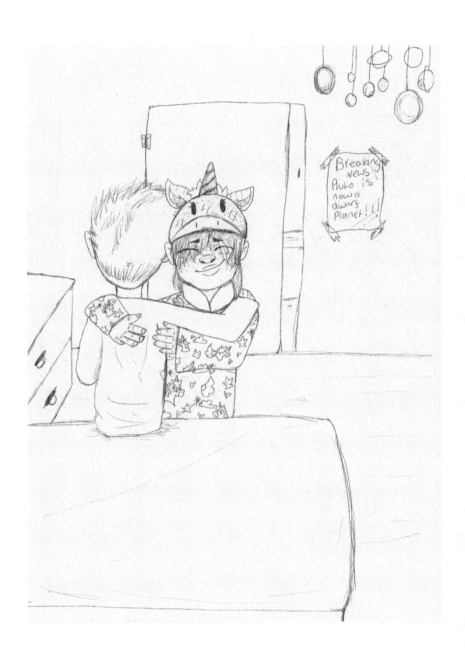

CHAPTER ELEVEN

Sunday morning Jake slept in for the first time in a long time. The week and his adventures in the fairy den must have caught up with him. It was 10 am before he opened his eyes. Sarah had slept in too. Rebekah was in the kitchen having a coffee when Jake ventured downstairs.

"My! Well hello!" She got up and planted a kiss on his forehead "Well that is a first, you must have needed that!" She walked over to get a bowl out for him and his favourite cereal "Sarah has only just got up too, that must have been some walk you guys went on yesterday"

"It was" Jake said sleepily as he sat down for his breakfast.

"Maybe next time I can come too?"

Jakes heart skipped a beat, he would love nothing more than to share this experience with his mum, but what if she thought it was dangerous and stopped them from going? His mind raced, as well as it could race having just woken up from a deep slumber.

"I'd love that Mum" He said truthfully "Let's take a picnic next week and spend the morning out"

"Ok" She looked happy and kissed Jake again on the forehead "I'll make us some lovely treats to take and even a cake as well"

The day was uneventful, Jake finished all of his homework, tidied his room (Not that it needed it much, Jake was pretty tidy anyway) and watched TV, Sarah popped in and out, sitting on his bed from time to time while she played with her dolls or watched a bit of TV with him, but other than that it was a lazy day: Just what he needed. His mind wandered back to their adventures yesterday, smiling every time he thought of it. Sarah was making her dolls fly with fairy dust up and down the hallway, she had named one of them Rowan.

Rebekah wanted to join them next time which meant they couldn't go; Jake loved them all three being together so he was happy they were going to have a picnic but he knew he would miss going to see the fairies too. Maybe if he got all his homework finished by Saturday him and Sarah could visit them on Sunday, the thought cheered him and he gazed out of his window that overlooked the field they crossed to get to the woods. He wondered what they were busy doing or gathering now before he settled down with his book about the planets. The smell of toast floated upstairs a few minutes before Rebekah appeared with cheese on toast for the both of them as a snack. He hated the crumbs on his bed but he loved cheese on toast and when they all sat together which they did right now, munching quietly and watching Jakes TV when blue planet came on with all wonderful sea creatures. Sarah nearly spat her toast out at the sight of some of them.

 "They are sooo weird! Look at what that one is doing!"

 They watched as a fish with a lightbulb hanging in front of him on a long muscle devoured its unsuspecting prey when the little fish were drawn to the light, not noticing the large fish behind it with long teeth snap shut around it.

"Woah" Sarah looked stunned "You wouldn't want to bump in to that on the beach"

 Jake laughed "You only find them in the deep parts of the ocean"

They sat and watched the rest of blue planet together, scrunched on Jakes bed, the plates (and crumbs) on the floor, arms round each other: content and happy.

CHAPTER TWELVE

Monday morning and Jake's anxiety was back; he could feel his panic rising as he entered the school grounds. Ahead of him were the usual crowd of followers that hung around Charlie like a bad smell. All ready and willing to do his bidding at the drop of a hat. He hadn't seen Charlie since that time outside of school, it still bothered him knowing what he saw and knowing that Charlie knew what he saw as well. It was undeniable, their eyes had locked on that day. Jake heard Charlies voice, familiar and spiteful. This time taunting one of his group, the rest all laughing along with him, probably relieved that for the moment it wasn't them on the receiving end.

Jake carried on walking at his usual pace and tried not to look up in case he caught Charlies eye, but when he did look up to see where he was going he found Charlie staring right at him. Jakes heart thumped loudly in his ears and then Charlie actually blushed and looked away. He had looked.....embarrassed. Jake was a little taken aback. The bell rang loudly, slowly breaking up the kids in their huddles to make their way to form room; Jake stayed behind as usual so he wasn't caught up in the rush.

All through his maths lesson (Which Charlie wasn't in thankfully) Jake thought about him, he tried to concentrate, but his mind wandered back to Charlie. He had never seen him look anything but angry or laughing at someone. To see him embarrassed had really surprised Jake. He tried to push it out of his mind and listen to his teacher. The sums on the board were fairly easy for Jake, he flew through them without too much trouble then it was time for his French lesson, suddenly announced by the shrill bell piercing his ears.

Everyone packed up their books, shoving them in to their bags as fast as they could, hoping to get out of a homework task if they were fast enough out of the lesson. Not so. Mr Bailey was a seasoned teacher and used to these tricks.

"Homework tonight!" He called loud enough to reach over the bubble of noise arising. A collective groan from around the room made Mr Bailey smile "Is to continue on page 32 of your workbooks and finish all questions. I need to see working out so you haven't used a calculator. Bye everyone, see you all on Thursday"

The hustle and bustle of changing lessons was something Jake had always hated. Everyone was switching classrooms at the same time, sometimes you had to go right to the other side of the school, it meant being quick and Jake didn't like shoving or being part of the rush, he liked to stay back and let others go. This meant he was always last to his lessons, last to sit down, last to get books out. Sometimes there would be a comment from the teacher or another pupil, sometimes the lesson had already started but always there would be stares.

Jake was concentrating on blocking out the noise, his head down, trying to keep to the flow of the movement between the corridor going; He was concentrating so much he didn't see Charlie coming the other way.. right for him.

Charlies shoulder connected with Jakes shoulder. Hard and deliberate. It pushed him back against the wall, shocked. When he looked up and saw Charlie, dread flooded through him. Charlie looked angry. His lips were squashed in to a thin line, his eyes narrowed and his hands were balled in to fists.

"Can I help you Mr Marden?" A familiar voice called from above the crowd. Mrs Pittman stepped in to Jakes eye sight and in between him and Charlie "What is going on here?!" She demanded looking right at Charlie as she did so

"Nothing Miss" Charlie's scowl didn't leave his face and he continued to stare at Jake.

"Jake?" Miss Pittman asked.

Jake simply stared at the floor.

"Right, if you're not going to talk, then I will have to guess." She looked back at Charlie "And I'm guessing that you were about to cause trouble AGAIN" She stepped closer to Charlie "You have only just come back from a suspension, so I suggest that if you don't want to repeat the experience you stay out of trouble and leave people alone." Mrs Pittman looked very stern, Jake had not seen her like this before. "Now go to your lesson Charlie".

The hall was quiet now, everyone had made their way to their lessons, Jake was definitely going to be late, the kind of late that he would get stares and comments as he found his chair. Once Charlie had walked away, Mrs Pittman turned to Jake,

"Is there anything you want to tell me Jake?"

Jake just stared at the floor and shook his head. Mrs Pittman sighed .

"Ok, you'd better hurry along to your lesson. You're already late."

Jake gathered up his bag he had dropped and began to walk away.

"Oh before you go! I have organised the lunchtime club in the library. Mr Geoffrey's is expecting you. There may also be a few other students attending but I'm not sure on those yet. All you have to do is turn up when its lunchtime and you've finished your lunch as there is no eating in the library"

Jake grinned, he was so relieved. Especially now with Charlie definitely wanting to seek him out, probably angry that he had seen what he had seen, even though that wasn't Jakes fault. He wanted to say thank you to Mrs Pittman, but the words wouldn't come out so instead he smiled his thanks to her. She nodded, seeming to understand, then pulled out a notepad from her bag and scribbled a few words on it before handing it to Jake .

"Take that to your teacher when you arrive, now go on you are very late"

Jake hurried off, trying to read the quick scrawl. It read: Needed a quick chat about a club, sorry to cause lateness then signed by Mrs Pittman. He took the steps two at a time at the next building and came through the door to find the lesson already in full flow. All eyes were on Jake but he tried to ignore them.

"Well hello at last." Mr's Peters voice sounded sarcastic when Jake walked in "You are quite late this time Jake, any explanation?"

Jake walked over to Mrs Peters and handed her the note. Her face softened as she read it.

"Ok, well please sit down and open your books, we are practising our words for the market today. Je voudrais une pomme sil vous plait. Now can anyone tell me what I just asked for?"

Hands shot up around the room as Jake sat down and organised himself, relieved he wasn't in trouble. Not with the teachers anyway, but it was breaktime afterwards and he had to try and stay out of Charlie's way. Jake couldn't concentrate. His stomach turning over and over. The beginnings of a headache threatened his temples, he took deep breaths to stay calm and try and focus but it was no use, his thoughts stayed on Charlie and as much as he willed it not to, the bell eventually sounded for break time and it was time to go outside.

Jake was as slow as he could possibly be packing up his books and leaving the classroom, he had to have wasted five minutes. He didn't want to hang around too long in the corridor, it would be too easy to be spotted so he decided to hide out in a cubicle in the boys toilets until the bell went. It was a long ten minutes to wait but finally the bell sounded and Jake waited one more minute before joining the corridor chaos for his next lesson, science.

Jake liked science, he found the experiments fascinating. He was a good pupil and his teacher liked him. It was a double lesson thankfully so he was safe until lunch time. Mr Green had the Bunsen burners already set up when they walked in. That always put the pupils in a good mood, knowing they were going to do something fun. They did the written work first, then the experiment. They were turning some liquid in to ammonia and by the time they had finished, everybody was exclaiming how much their new liquid smelled of wee. Jake had to work alongside Harjinda: She was a nice quiet girl and they didn't need to talk to share the bunsen burner, they naturally took turns, handing each other the test tube to smell afterwards. The lesson went quick, too quick and before he knew it Mr Green was giving them their five minute reminder to pack their things away to get ready for the bell. The bell Jake was dreading. He was hungry and wanted his lunch but he knew the library would be safe, he decided to skip his lunch and go straight to the library so he didn't see Charlie.

Jake was quicker than usual when the bell sounded, he wasn't pushing to get out like everybody else but he didn't hang around either. Taking quick steps around the huddle of people from his classroom he rounded the corner of the canteen, just needed to get to reception and up the stairs.

Charlies fist seemed to come out of nowhere, slamming in to Jakes chin. It didn't hurt at first, he felt stunned when he fell on to the ground, then realised what was happening and what was going to happen. He covered his head instinctively and waited, when nothing happened he looked up to see Mrs Pittman holding Charlies sleeve in a tight fist, preventing him from hitting Jake again. She looked very angry.

"What on earth are you doing?!" turning a deep shade of red in anger. "I have had enough of your nonsense boy!" She stepped in between Jake and Charlie, letting go of his sleeve "Now get to the head masters office now. MOVE!"

Jake had never seen Mrs Pittman lose her temper. Ever. He may have been more surprised at that than what Charlie had just done.

She turned around and took several deep breaths "Come on Jake up you get. Are you ok?" There was quite a crowd around them now, mostly disappointed that it hadn't turned in to a full blown fight.

"Go and eat your lunch in the library this once Jake, tell Mr Geoffrey's I said it was ok" Jake looked down, knowing he wouldn't be able to pass on the message. "Hang on, wait." Mrs Pittman delved in to the big black bag she always had on her: Jake often wondered how someone so small could lug around something so big all day. But for someone so small (Mrs Pittman was about 4 foot 10) she had a mighty voice when she wanted to he had just learned. She scrawled on a piece of paper and handed it to Jake.

"Give this to Mr Geoffrey's. I'll be up soon to have a chat with you"

The crowd had dispersed by then and Jake wasted no time in heading to the library. His chin had begun to throb and he wondered if he would get a bruise. He stole a look at the note before entering the library: " I have given Jake permission to eat in the library today under special circumstances. Will explain later. Mrs P"

The library had two big, heavy, wooden doors; they closed softly behind him, seeming to shut out the sound from outside. The smell of the books was welcoming; it was so calm and quiet in here, Jake felt himself finally start to relax a little. He hadn't realised he was holding his shoulders up so high and tense until the sides of his neck began to ache. Relief that he was finally here in the sanctity of the library was so great he had an overwhelming urge to cry. Jake knew that any attempt at speaking or trying to communicate would result in tears falling down his face so he concentrated hard on keeping them in, his throat aching with unshed tears and slowly approached Mr Geoffrey's who had noticed him coming in and was waiting patiently at his desk. Jake produced the note Mrs Pittman had given him and handed it to him, looking down so he wouldn't see how close to tears Jake was.

Mr Geoffrey's was a kind man with a quiet gravelly voice. He had white hair that stuck up all manner of ways, a white moustache and round glasses. He wore a woollen vest over a shirt and had a large belly.

"Go on and find yourself a seat Lad and enjoy your lunch"

Jake walked over to the quietest spot in the corner of the library he could find, dropping his bag and sitting down heavily in a chair. He wasn't hungry anymore, he just wanted the day to end and go home. He tried to think of the fairies, remembering the bottle he kept in his pocket but even that didn't lift his spirits.

What had he ever done to Charlie? Deep down he knew he was angry because of what he had seen.. but that wasn't Jakes fault Charlies Mum had hit him like that. Why take it out on him?

Jake thought of how happy he had been only yesterday, how happy he had been last week in school when he made great progress talking to

Mrs Pittman and showing he wasn't willing to do drama to Mrs Laindon, both times good things came of it and now here he was feeling like it was never going to get better for him here.

Sadness enveloped him like a heavy blanket pulling him down. He couldn't stop the tears now and he didn't care either. He wasn't sure how long he had been sat there like that, just staring at the ground letting his tears fall but he started to hear voices and recognised Mrs Pittman asking Mr Geoffrey's where Jake was.

"Took himself in that corner he did. Looked very down"

Mrs Pittman found Jake and dragged a chair over to him, she sat down and put her arm around him, handing him a tissue.

"That boy is a trouble maker Jake, he always finds someone to pick on. Don't worry he won't get away with it. He is at the head masters office now and after all he has done this school year I do believe they will put him on suspension again" She sighed deeply "They may even expel him this time"

Jakes head snapped up. Expel him? Jake would love more than anything never to see Charlie again but he couldn't help wondering how on earth Charlies Mum would react if he was expelled and more to the point what she would do. He knew he shouldn't care after what he had just done, but he couldn't get the image out of his head.

"I've called your Mum Jake. She is on her way to pick you up. Although I understand she wants to have a word with the headmaster first"

Jake nodded, relieved. He didn't think he would be able to face his next lesson without breaking in to tears again. Mrs Pittman sat with him in silence until his Mum arrived. The library was on the second level of the school overlooking the carpark and they saw her coming, walking briskly towards the school with a determined look on her face.

Mrs Pittman stood up "I'll fetch your Mum Jake, stay here for a moment please"

Mrs Pittman hurried out of the library, leaving Jake. He watched as a moment later she came in to view and approached Rebekah. Jake couldn't hear what was being said but he could tell it was heated. Rebekah looked upset and angry. Mrs Pittman seemed to be doing her best to calm her down, their exchange continued for a few more minutes before they began heading towards the school again.

"Jake?" A few minutes later his Mum and Mrs Pittman were in the library. Just seeing her brought fresh tears he simply couldn't hold back "Oh come here" She embraced him, his head nuzzled in to the soft cotton of her top, her familiar perfume just as comforting as her hug. When they pulled apart, Jake could see she too, was upset.

"Listen, I've got to talk to the head master about that awful boy. Hopefully they will expel him this time and you never have to see him again. It isn't the first time he has caused you trouble is it." She delved in to her giant handbag (Jake and Sarah always teased her about it) pulling out her bundle of keys.

"Here, you go and sit in the car. I'm not sure how long I will be. Ok?" Rebekah kissed him on the forehead, Jake could already feel himself relax a little and he made his way out of the library and to the carpark to find the car. Jake spotted the red Fiesta easily. Unlocking the car and climbing in, the car smelled of those hanging things you buy at the petrol stations which Jake hated when they were new and had that overpowering smell, but this one had been there for months so wasn't as offensive. He sat down and closed his eyes, wondering if Charlie was still in the headmasters office. At that moment a black car rumbled up quickly behind him, music so loud, he could feel it in the car in front.

Jake recognised the blonde woman when she stepped out of the car immediately. It was Charlies Mother. She looked so angry, it made Jake sit back in fear. He watched her approach the school slowly, looking around like a predator.

The lunch bell had already gone and all pupils were back in class now, everything was quiet. He hoped and hoped his mum would come out first so they could drive away without him having to see Charlie at all. His eyes trained on the door leading to reception where they would come out of. Each time it opened, he sat up in anticipation of it being his Mum. Each time it was another teacher hurrying to another part of the school for their lesson, occasionally it was a pupil. Once it was a pupil and their Dad, clearly going home unwell: The young girl looked almost green and her Dad was carrying her bags, walking slowly with her leaning on his arm.

The next time the door opened, it swung open so hard the metal hit the post behind it causing a loud BANG. Jake's head snapped up, his heart beat loudly in his chest and his stomach turned over and over as he saw Charlie being marched out of school by his Mum. Charlie's head was down; He looked like he had been crying, his mother's face screwed up tightly and red. She had him by the scruff of his jacket and was yanking him every time he fell a step behind. Jake wanted to hide, but he had nowhere to go. Their car was directly behind where Jake sat in his mums car, they would have to walk past him. He started to slide down in his seat, scared of what would happen if he was seen. Charlie's mum was frightening. They passed his car, Jakes heart beat pounded in his ears but he remained still. He could just see their bodies pass by, looking in to the rear view mirror he knew they were at their car now. He hoped they would get in it quickly and drive away but then instead of getting in straight away, Charlies Mum literally threw him to the ground, his face ground against the stones on the path.

"Idiot boy!" His Mum hissed at him through clenched teeth "What did I tell you? Get up!"

Jake watched on in horror as Charlie fumbled to his feet, his chin bleeding from being scraped on the ground. He had his eyes closed and his head bent, he seemed to know what was coming when his Mum delivered the first blow. It sent him flying backwards on to the ground again, blood trickled out of his mouth and he lay there for a second before his Mum grabbed his shoulder, pulling him to his feet. She hit him again, this time in the stomach. Charlie doubled over, winded. She then opened the car door and pushed him backwards inside until he was completely in then she slammed the door.

Jake felt sick. He wanted to scream "STOP!" He wanted to get this vicious woman off him, he didn't care what he had done. Charlie looked small and frightened. But he couldn't, he was rooted to the chair in fear and astonishment. Eyes now fixed in the rear view mirror. Charlies Mum heaved herself in the car and started the engine, but before she drove away, she looked at him in disgust one more time and slapped his face. She was yelling but Jake couldn't hear what she was saying. Jake held his face in his hands, tears coursing down his cheeks: This time not for him but for Charlie who seemed like just a scared kid with an awful Mother.

When Rebekah got back to the car, she thought the fresh tears were about what had happened earlier, she leaned over, putting her warm soft hands over Jakes. Hands that would never have struck him, hands that wiped away his tears, hands that had tucked him in, applied plasters, made his favourite meals. Charlie didn't have that he realised all of a sudden, understanding more why he was so angry all the time.

He looked down, tears still falling, his nose now blocked.

"Hey, come on. It's going to be ok. They are having a meeting tomorrow afternoon about what to do with Charlie and they can't tell me for sure but they strongly hinted that he is going to be expelled this time and you will never have to see him again" Rebekah looked in to Jakes eyes, concern and love for him clear for Jake to see "Ok?"

Jake couldn't speak, or do anything. He just hung his head and stayed that way until they got home.

"I'm going to need to pick Sarah up, do you want to come with me or do you want to put the telly on for a bit?" Rebekah stroked his hair out of his face and hugged him "I'll pick up some pizza on the way home"

 "I'll stay here" Jake replied hoarsely, his throat still sore from crying.

 "Ok. Well, get comfy and I'll see you soon" She kissed Jake gently on the forehead, picked up her car keys and left.

 Before the car had left the driveway, Jake had written a quick note so his Mum wouldn't worry telling her he had gone for a walk, left through the back door, making sure to lock it after him and run over to the fields as fast as he could. He just hoped they knew he was coming. He wiped his tears furiously away and headed for the woods.

CHAPTER THIRTEEN

They did know he was coming. Jake didn't hesitate and take his time when he entered the woods this time, he went straight to the tree trunk stump, wishing for the portal to be open for him, relief flooded his body when he saw the glimmer of colour there and leaned in to it. His body rolled over softly in the pile of leaves and he sat up quickly, looking around. There was Raven as he hoped she would be, ready to guide him to the big Oak tree. He wondered how they knew, they must sense him coming.

"Jake" Raven flitted towards him. She was different, she had a troubled look about her this time. Jake realised it was for him.

"Are you ok?"

Jake looked down at his hands, he felt so many things. Sadness for what had happened between him and Charlie, guilt for not getting out of his car and stopping what was happening and fear for not knowing what to do next.

"You don't have to speak, come on Madelaine's expecting you" She rubbed her hands together, a cloud of gold dust appearing between her delicate hands, then blew it gently over Jake. He felt the familiar lift of lightlessness surround him and they flew silently together towards the big Oak tree.

"Come" Raven ushered Jake inside, he didn't want to see anyone else, didn't think he could talk to anyone else. Raven must have known and she simply led him immediately upwards towards Madelaine's room.

She was waiting for him already on her chair and gestured for him to sit down opposite her.

"Thank you Raven, please do sit down Jake"

Jake sat down as Raven flew back down to the bottom of the Oak tree. There was already a cup of brew ready for him at the table.

"You knew I was coming." It was a statement rather than a question.

"Of course" Madelaine leaned forward: Her kindly face reaching in to Jakes eyes, she took his hands in to her own. They were so small and delicate, yet they felt strong. Her white hair cascaded around her shoulders, she was like light itself; her calm, gentle nature helping to balance Jakes anxious mind and stomach. Jake waited for her to speak, when she didn't he realised it was him who needed to talk, it was after all why he had come here.

"I don't know what to do " He eventually confessed.

Madelaine nodded, seeming to understand, patient as ever in letting Jake go at his own pace.

"I hated him so much earlier after he hit me, he'd made me so afraid to even walk around school and I think it was because I saw his mum hit him the other week. That wasn't my fault I saw that. I WISH I hadn't!" Jake emphasised. "Why did it make him so angry at me?"

"Sometimes when people have seemed strong to others, then are seen as vulnerable they can feel threatened or even weak, Then they feel the need to show they are as strong as always. Strength comes in many forms and Charlie has it confused with control and bullying. Those that are happy on the inside do not behave the way that Charlie does."

Jake nodded, that did make sense, but it wasn't fair at all.

"After Mrs Pittman said he may get expelled I was so relieved I would never have to see him again. Then I was waiting for my mum and –"

Jake broke off and covered his face in his hands.

"I'm such a coward" He whispered.

"Jake you are not a coward" Madelaine said with conviction. "How could you know how to react to seeing something so terrible? How do you feel now?"

"Scared."

"Why?"

"Because I know it's the right thing to say something and tell someone, but what will happen If I do?" Jake searched Madelaine's face for answers

"I think Jake, the question needs to be; what will happen if you don't?"

The image of Charlie; small and frightened being thrown down on to the ground in the carpark and beaten by his mum made Jake shudder. No one deserved that. No one.

The realisation that he HAD to tell someone gave way to fresh anxiety about how, when speaking was one of his biggest obstacles in school... and what would Charlie do to him when he spoke out? Especially if today was anything to go by.

"Jake, Charlie may be unable to do that for himself" It was as if she had read his mind.

"I don't know how I can"

"We are all stronger than we know and strength comes in many, many forms. Certainly not fists. Your strength is in here" She placed her warm hand on Jakes chest "And it will guide you. Trust it"

Jake nodded, he knew what he had to do and Madelaine was right if he didn't speak out what would happen to Charlie. The thought came, one which would plague him until the morning; If his mum could do that in a school carpark what was she like at home?

"I have to go" Jake stood up. Almost immediately Raven appeared, ready to take him back.

"You can do this Jake. I believe in you"

He smiled weakly back at Madelaine. He wished he believed in himself as much as she did.

"Thank you for listening"

"Always Jake, always."

Raven blew a fresh cloud of gold dust over him and guided him back to the door, they flew in silence, a sober air between them. Once they reached the tree stump, Raven turned to Jake.

"You are stronger than you know, focus on your strength Jake. We will see you soon"

"Bye Raven"

Jake stepped through the portal and POP he was normal size laying on the ground, staring up at the trees and hearing the birds chirping happily. He knew what he had to do and there was no time to waste. Jake ran home all the way, he burst in to the kitchen as Rebekah was unloading shopping bags.

"Hey Love, I read your note. Are you ok?"

"Mum I need to talk to you. It's important"

CHAPTER FOURTEEN

Rebekah sank in to the kitchen chair in astonishment. Jake opposite her, had told her everything. Silence stretched between them like an elastic band waiting to be broken.

"And you're sure of this" Rebekah looked up at him, hoping he wasn't sure, knowing he was. Jake wouldn't even think of saying such things otherwise.

"Yes Mum. I wish it wasn't true but it is. His Mum hurt him badly and I saw it all" He looked down at his hands "And I didn't stop it" He muttered guiltily.

"Hey!" Rebekah's head snapped up "Don't do that" She ordered reaching for his hand across their cosy wooden table "You are not responsible for what happened and how could you have physically stopped her Jake? I have seen her she is a formidable woman. You are doing what you can right now, telling me about it and together we can help the boy."

"How?" Jake enquired

"Do you know where he lives?"

Jake shook his head "No Mum we're not friends"

"Then we have to go to the school with what you've seen." She glanced at the clock 4:35 "I'll try them now"

Rebekah picked up their phone from the wall and dialled the school's number. Jake could tell the options were taking her to voicemail by the frustration in her face as she replaced the receiver.

"We will have to speak to them in the morning, This really isn't the sort of thing I can leave over voicemail" Her forehead creased together and she rubbed her eyes "That poor boy. It doesn't excuse how he has been treating you Jake, but at least now we can understand a little. They say all bullies have a bully and she is clearly his one"

"What's for dinner Mum? I'm starving! Jake I got 100% in my maths test today! We learned that eyelashes last about 150 days and our fingernails grow four times as fast as toenails! That's mad isn't it!" Sarah grabbed a cookie off the side and took a large bite "What's for dinner Mum?" bits of cookie sprayed across the table and she waited for Rebekah to answer. Normally Rebekah would admonish her for speaking with her mouthful but she simply smiled and tucked Sarah's once tidy hair behind her ears.

"Pizza"

"Yes!" Sarah air punched the air, skipping out of the room, spinning in a circle every third step.

"Where on earth does she get that energy from?" Rebekah shook her head and her and Jake shared a smile of fondness for Sarah. She was a constant source of activity, it left people dizzy trying to keep up but she always lightened the mood.

"I'll put dinner on" Rebekah went on autopilot; she needed to cook dinner, although she didn't think she could eat any of it. She felt sick inside knowing what Charlie was going through and they needed to help him. A thought occurred to her and she turned to face Jake.

"They are going to be asking you a lot of questions tomorrow when we go to the school about this"

Jake nodded, he knew exactly what his Mum meant. Questions he would find hard to answer because he rarely spoke. He had already thought of this and had a plan in his mind.

"I'm going to write everything down. They will probably ask me to do that anyway won't they? I know when there was a fight at school before both the kids had to write a statement, I heard one of them talking about it in class"

Rebekah nodded, some of the concern lifting away, she sat next to Jake "I'm so proud of you. So, so proud. This boy has caused you some miserable times at school and here you are helping him now"

Jake looked down, he didn't feel proud of himself. He didn't say anything the first time he saw Charlies mum hit him outside of the shop that day. Rebekah must have read his mind.

"Listen" She cupped his chin with her hand, lifting his face up to look at her "Nobody wants to believe these things go on and seeing it for the first time must have been quite a shock"

"It was" He nodded "And I think that's why he hit me today. It was his first day back after being suspended for a week"

"I think you're right and he was wrong to hit you. He is a very angry boy" She sighed, looking troubled "And now we know why, we must do the right thing. Well done Jake for speaking out" She held him tight then, emotion ebbing through both of them "It's going to be ok".

Jake didn't do his homework that night, him and his mum both agreed he should only work on his statement of what had happened for the morning. He couldn't eat his dinner, just a few mouthfuls and sleep seemed impossible. Jake could not stop thinking about Charlie and what he had to do. His stomach flipped and turned all night: he lost count of how many times he turned his pillow over, looked at his clock and worked out how many hours he had until he had to get up. Jake finally fell in to a fitful sleep around 3 am, the alarm bolting him awake at 6:30, the first thought in his mind was his task ahead. How was he going to do this? What if they ask him questions he hadn't written down? What if they didn't believe him? What if Charlie heard he had told and was even more angry then did to Jake what Charlies mum did to him?

"Morning!" Still dressed in unicorn cotton pajamas, holding Betsy the doll: Sarah came in and flopped on the bed, arms round Jake. She yawned loudly , farted, giggled then left. Despite the situation Jake found himself in, he laughed and hid under the covers to avoid the smell she had left behind.

"You're gross"

"I know!" She said proudly from the hallway.

Jake's bed had never seemed more comfortable than this moment when he detested the thought of moving from it, through tiredness and not wanting to face what was ahead. He closed his heavy eyes, pulled the duvet close around him, drifting back off to sleep.

He was gently woken up again by his mum 30 minutes later with a cup of tea. Rebekah was already dressed and sitting on his bed. She was pretty his mum; her hair was tied up in a clip with little tendrils falling loose either side of her face. She wore jeans and a blue blouse with sandals and by the looks of things she didn't sleep well either last night.

"Hey" She said setting his cup down on his bedside table.

"You didn't sleep well did you?"

"No." Jake sat up, rubbing his eyes. They itched.

"Well drink this, I've put some sugar in it and we will take Sarah to school. You're not going in today, let's just focus on talking to Mr Mumford, then we will come home and you can go back to sleep ok?"

Jake nodded, reaching for his tea.

"Jake's not going in? Are you sick Jake?" Sarah looked concerned overhearing their conversation.

"Yeah I'm sick. Your farts have poisoned me"

They all burst out laughing, then Sarah did it again, this time lifting her leg when she knew it was coming

"My God Sarah!" Rebekah covered her mouth and nose "What have you eaten?!"

"Pizza! And lots of it" She grinned and they both knew she was getting ready for another one. They were right and it stank. Jake threw the covers over him and Rebekah cried "Nooo!"

"Don't judge me!" Sarah sounded offended "It is a natural bodily function. Besides I have to get rid of it all before I go to school... can you imagine! I'd have no friends left, I'd gas them all!" Sarah laughed at her own joke then run off to finish getting ready.

Jake was still laughing when he tried to drink his tea. Sarah was such a tonic, she lifted them up just by being her and already he felt better, although his room had a bad odour to it now.

"Let's go!" Rebekah was waiting in the car, Sarah was faffing around indoors trying to find something, after locating it, she emerged from the house then ran back inside past Jake.

"What is she doing now?" Rebekah asked exasperated.

"She's in the loo mum"

"Oh" Rebekah nodded "Good"

They said goodbye to Sarah when they pulled up outside her school. She didn't want either of them getting out to walk her in. She could do it by herself she said. It was strange to think that in two years Sarah would be at Jakes school as well, he kind of looked forward to that: He liked her crazy chatter and her whirlwind ways, but she was equally soft and tuned in to Jakes moods. It would help Rebekah out too, they would be able to walk to and from school together so she could go to work that bit earlier and get an extra hour in she said.

 Watching her walk through the gates was bitter sweet; different friends flocked to her once she was in sight. She greeted them all warmly and with excitement, it was infectious and he could see why she was so well liked, she made people feel good. Made people smile. They hurried off towards the school building and out of sight, ready to start another adventure of the day. It was a totally different way to how Jakes school day was, he didn't have one friend. It would have been good to have a friend but he wouldn't know what to say and he didn't play really, that just wasn't his way. He read books, liked nature walks, documentaries and school work. He would just be happy to get through each school day without the fear of becoming overwhelmed by the constant noise, noise he felt he could drown in.

 The engine rumbled gently as Rebekah turned the key again, breaking Jake from his thoughts. Sarah was such a good distraction, now she was gone and they were headed for his school, he felt sick. He didn't know if he could do this, his head began to throb and all the possible outcomes ran through his head, the same ones that had kept him awake for most of the night.

Rebekah reached down and took his hand, sensing his anxieties.

"We do this together Jake"

He nodded. After kissing his hand and replacing it in his lap, she drove them slowly to school.

Thankfully, the rush had gone, most kids were now in class, there were only a few stragglers left hurrying to their form room. Rebekah parked their well loved and used fiesta in the same carpark as she had the day before: Jake immediately having flashbacks of what he had seen. It took all his strength to get out of the car and walk with his Mum towards reception, the electric doors welcoming them as they swung open on their approach.

Mrs March was on the desk busy looking through forms and counting money. She was heavily made up with blonde hair tied in a tight bun, long fingernails painted dark red. Jake wondered how on earth she could even pick up the coins, but she did it expertly and held one finger up without looking up in a gesture for them to wait a moment. She wrote down her amount then looked up and smiled.

"Good morning. How can I help you?"

"We would like to see Mr Mumford please" Rebekah said, Jake watched as Mrs March frowned.

"Do you have an appointment?"

"No but-"

"Then I'm afraid you'll have to make an appointment. Mr Mumford is very busy" Mrs March reached for her appointment book, her long fingernails curling round it.

"This is very important and we need to see him right away" Rebekah insisted.

"They are all very important Miss..?"

"Listen" Rebekah leaned forward so her face was almost inside the screen opening that separated them "We are here about a very serious safe guarding incident involving one of the pupils on the school grounds and I insist on seeing him right away for that persons safety"

Mrs March's fingers froze around the file as Rebekah's words took effect.

"I see" She let go of the file, instead now both hands pushed her chair back from the desk that faced them. "Excuse me for one minute please"

Mrs March left the room, towards the offices behind them. Jake knew that was the head masters office. By now he was trembling, feeling sick and had pains gnawing at his insides, Rebekah sensed his unease and put his arm around him.

"It's going to be ok Jake. " She assured him quietly. The large clock behind Mrs March's desk ticked on annoyingly each second that passed. It seemed they were waiting for hours but it was two and a half minutes; Jake counted.

Mr Mumford came out from the door Mrs March had disappeared in to. He was so tall he filled the doorway, Mr Mumford always wore a blue suit with a blue tie, he was slim with a large nose. Jake had never really met him before, just seen him in the assemblies although Jake never paid attention to anything that was being said.

"Mrs Booth, would you and Jake like to come through to my office please" He smiled and Jake thought his smile was stretchy, he seemed to have too much skin for his face, but when he did smile, his eyes did too. He looked nice and kind but serious.

Rebekah and Jake walked through the reception office and through the back room to where Mr Mumford's office was. He had a large desk organised with files and a paperweight holding them in place with a big window behind it letting in the bright summer sun. In front of his desk was a small grey sofa that could sit two people and a comfortable grey chair, in between them both was an oval table. It was a very neat and ordered room, Jake liked it, it smelled of polish.

"Sit down Mrs Booth, Jake."

Jake and Rebekah sat on the sofa together while Mr Mumford took the chair, he seemed far too big for it and leaned forward, elbows on his knees, putting his hands together.

"Thank you for coming to see me today. I hear you had an upsetting day yesterday Jake, how are you feeling now?"

Jake's stomach flipped, his heart beat loudly in his throat and he stared at the floor. He couldn't speak. Buzzing started in his ears and he began to lose focus of the room.

Rebekah took his hand telling him it was alright and to breathe slowly. He could hear his mum explaining his difficulties to Mr Mumford but it was fuzzy as he focused on his breathing: count in 5 breaths, then count out 7 breaths. Rebekah had taught him how to get hold of his thoughts that way, he would focus so much on the counting that everything else faded away until he felt better.

A few minutes later Jake felt like he was back in the room again.

"I'm aware of what happened yesterday with Charlie and Jake yesterday as we spoke Mrs Booth when you came to collect Jake" Mr Mumford began.

Rebekah realised that he thought that was why they had come today "Yes, but we are here for a different reason today. I would have rung yesterday but it was too late and I didn't want to leave this type of message on the phone."

Mr Mumford's brow furrowed in confusion and concern.

"Yesterday as I was collecting Jake and came in to see you, something happened on the school grounds that Jake witnessed and it was very unpleasant"

Mr Mumford nodded for Rebekah to continue.

"Charlies mother came to collect him as well and when they were at the carpark she hit him several times, hurting him quite badly. Jake saw it all"

Mr Mumford sat up straight; breathing in deeply. His face screwed up, he wrung his hands then let out his breath. "Ok" He pulled his chair forward a little towards Jake and lowered his voice to a much softer tone, leaning forwards, his large warm hand gently touched Jakes wrist; the action made Jake look straight up at him. Mr Mumford wasn't scary, he looked nice but worried. Jake nodded slowly, his voice dried up again and he opened his mouth but nothing came out. Rebekah handed Mr Mumford the statement Jake had written the night before, he scanned the first few lines then turned to Jake again "Did you write this Jake?"

Again Jake nodded, he willed his voice out but nothing. Jake watched as Mr Mumford read his statement, all the while battling within to speak and say yes I saw it yes I wrote that. The plug was winning, tears welled up in Jakes eyes.. he furiously wiped them away, angry at himself. He thought of Charlie and what he had seen, of Charlie's mum the way she hit him and coldly got him in the car, he thought of the words she had used on him, the same words Charlie had used on Jake and knew Charlie was scared too. To speak, to say what he wanted, Charlie had his own plug and somebody needed to speak for him too.

"Yes" Jake croaked, his mouth dry "I saw it all and I wrote that"

Mr Mumford stopped reading and smiled at Jake, he leaned forward seeing how difficult that was for him.

"Thank you Jake. This is a very serious allegation so I have to be absolutely clear and sure that what you have written has come from you which is why I asked. You and your mum stay here, I will ask Mrs March to bring us some coffee and water and I may have to ask you to speak to somebody else Jake, just what you have told me that you wrote this because we need to report it straight away. Ok?"

Both Rebekah and Jake nodded, Mr Mumford left the room then with Jakes statement.

"I'm so very proud of you Jake" Rebekah put her arms around him, kissing his forehead. Jake felt tired, he wanted to go home and close his eyes.

That morning was a long one. Whoever Mr Mumford had to speak to took a while, he had Mrs March come in with coffees, water and biscuits as he took the phone call. It seemed to take forever but eventually Mr Mumford came back. He looked tired too now and rubbed his forehead as he sat down, reaching for his cold coffee.

"Well I have spoken to a lady who is on her way over. Her name is Joan Simmond's and she would like to speak with you Jake about what you have seen and then I'm sure you'll be happy to know you're free to go home and relax."

Jake couldn't wait to go, the build up of his anxieties, his lack of sleep and the waiting around had caught up with him, he felt so tired, shoulders sagging Jake nodded, leaning against Rebekah.

"You have done really well Jake, it couldn't have been easy to speak out and I know that you do find speaking especially difficult"

Mr Mumford walked over to his desk, picking up his phone he pressed one of the numbers and waited a moment.

"Mrs March would you bring in some fresh coffee please? Thank you"

They waited another 30 minutes and Mrs March tapped on the door announcing Joan Simmond's arrival. She was a short blonde woman with lots of make up. She Wore a long green dress, the kind of green Jake loved, it reminded him of the forest. She was carrying files and a professional smile, she must have already known Mr Mumford as she nodded her hello.

Mr Mumford brought over another chair which Joan took gratefully after shaking Rebekah's and Jakes hand.

"Coffee Joan?"

"Oh yes please, two sugars"

Mr Mumford picked up his phone again to request more coffee, Rebekah declined this time and Joan organised her paperwork on her lap. Jake began to feel anxious again, his stomach turning over. Was he expected to say everything he had seen? He didn't think he would be able to.

While they waited for yet more coffee, Joan introduced herself to Rebekah and Jake.

"Hi, I'm Joan" She smiled warmly at them both.

"I'm Rebekah, this is Jake"

"Hello Rebekah, Hello Jake"

Jake smiled and Joan focused her attention on him

"I want to thank you for being so brave and telling your mum and Mr Mumford about what you have seen. Now would you be able to tell me more about that? Where abouts on the school ground did it happen?"

Jake realised she was asking direct questions, his throat began to clam up, he didn't know what to say next and his stomach started to hurt.

Rebekah sat forward a little "Jake finds it quite difficult to speak in front of people he doesn't know. He stayed up late last night writing out exactly what he has seen and how it happened"

Mr Mumford stepped forward, handing Joan the letter which she scanned quickly.

"I see" Although she looked a little bewildered "The thing is, I have to speak to Jake to make sure he is the one that saw this and these are his words"

"Well maybe you could read what he has written and ask him some yes or no questions?" Rebekah offered.

Joan thought for a moment, then nodded.

"Ok, let's start with that"

Joan sat back to read Jakes statement, it was silent in the room except for the crinkling of the paper as she turned it over to read the other side. The clock ticked loudly in the room. It was now 11.15.

Joan finished reading and put down the letter at 11:26, she picked up her coffee and had a long gulp, picked up her notebook and pen, then looked at Jake. She smiled without it reaching her eyes.

"That couldn't have been easy to witness Jake"

Jake remembered how helpless he felt at the time and tears welled up in his eyes. He looked down not wanting anybody to see.

"I understand this is very difficult but you've done an amazing thing coming forward to tell people what happened. You're doing the right thing and you are helping Charlie right now by telling me the truth"

Jake looked up, Rebekah held his hand tightly, encouraging him. He nodded, tears escaped down his cheeks as he whispered "I wanted to help. I was scared" The words were barely a whisper but they were there and they all heard them. Rebekah wanted to hug him tightly and whirl him around the room, her heart almost bursting with pride at his words but sad that these words were so painful to say. Instead she sat still and allowed Jake the time to go at his own pace.

"I bet you were, that's not easy to witness, let alone know what to do. I can see this is hard for you and you are doing amazing Jake you really are. I will accept these are your words if you just tell me you wrote this"

"I wrote the letter, I saw everything" Jakes words came out between tears but they came.

Joan smiled and this time her eyes crinkled at the sides, it made her look younger.

"Thank you Jake"

"What happens now? Rebekah wanted to know.

"Well now we have to investigate and interview, so you're work is done. Leave it with us"

"Will Charlie be ok?" Rebekah asked

"First we need to investigate, then if we feel Charlie is in a dangerous situation we will look in to alternative care for him but we will move quickly. He is suspended at the moment isn't he?" Joan looked to Mr Mumford for confirmation.

"Yes he is" Mr Mumford said, his chin resting in his hands as he listened to all going on in the room.

"Ok, well Jake, you are free to go home now. You've done really well speaking to us and we will handle it from here" Joan smiled kindly at them both "Take care"

"Thank you, good bye" Rebekah reached for her handbag while Mr Mumford opened the door, he followed them through and began walking them to the carpark.

"I just want you to show me where it happened so I can check the CCTV as well"

"I've parked in the same place as yesterday so It must have been here. Jake?"

Jake nodded, remembering it all again.

"Ok lad. Thank you again. You don't need to worry anymore ok. You have done the right thing, I'm proud of you"

Jake looked up to Mr Mumford's face towering above him. He was used to his mum telling him she was proud of him, that was kind of her job wasn't it. But the head master? For the first time in two days Jake started to feel a little better and he smiled. He had done the right thing and it wasn't as scary as he thought it was going to be, they listened to him, they really listened. But he was so, so tired now, the lack of sleep, worry of speaking out and the stress of yesterday caught up with him; Jake longed for the solace of his bedroom to just be alone for a while.

Mr Mumford shook both their hands before turning to go back to his office.

Rebekah and Jake climbed in to the car, exhausted and ready to go home.

"You ready?"

Jake nodded.

"I know I have said this before but I am so proud of you Jake. You did the right thing today and you've helped that boy, even though he has been so terribly mean to you, you still did the right thing" Rebekah smoothed his hair back a little which he usually hated but this time he didn't mind, then kissed his forehead gently "I love you"

"Love you too Mum"

"Right, let's go get you some lunch, how does tomato soup with a crusty roll and lots of butter sound?"

"Sounds perfect"

After lunch, Jake put his comfortable blue cotton pajamas on, turned on his TV and climbed in to bed, he intended to watch blue planet but instead he fell asleep and only woke up at the smell of Rebekah's cooking, it smelled like bolognaise (One of Jake's favourites).

"At last!" Sarah threw herself on the bed "Mum told me to be quiet so you could rest. Man you can sleep for England! How did you wangle another day off? Are you sick?" Sarah sat up and tested his forehead with the back of her hand, Jake stayed quiet, he knew from experience she didn't really need her questions answered "Guess what happened to me today? " Sarah jumped up, standing in front of him, her hair a total mess sticking out from all angles. Nothing like the neat French plait mum sent her to school with that morning then she farted really loudly and she laughed "Not that, but wow I wanted to ALL DAY!" She wiggled her bum around "Oh it stinks!

Anyway, guess what happened? I fell over in front of everyone!" She paused for dramatic effect "Everyone! On my face Jake. It was soooo embarrassing"

"Good job you didn't fart then eh, THAT would have been embarrassing" Jake laughed.

"Yeah" She agreed seriously. "Mum is cooking spaghetti bolognaise, with garlic bread and a mountain of cheese. I love cheese. Are you getting up? It's nearly ready. In fact, you stay there and I'll get the first pick on the garlic bread"

Jake jumped up "Right get out of my way!"

"No chance, I'm quicker than you!"

"Definitely smellier"

They raced downstairs pushing, shoving and laughing as Rebekah dished up their dinner, it turned out there was extra garlic bread anyway but they ate every bit and listened to Sarah's constant stream of chatter about her day, she only paused now and again to eat. As usual she was last to finish because she simply could not stop talking.

"I got told off today as well" She said sulkily as Rebekah cleared away hers and Jakes plates, they had finished and Sarah still had a long way to go

"Did you? What for?"

"Talking!" Sarah exclaimed indignantly.

Jake burst out laughing "Oh well that's just not like you is it?"

Thanks to Sarah, the mood had lifted at home and Jake felt happy again.

He dreamed that night of flying, really flying. Soaring through the skies as high as the birds. Wind rushing against his skin as he dipped and dived, free and without worries.

CHAPTER FIFTEEN

 School was different the next day. Jake didn't expect he would see Charlie so he didn't have the worry of bumping in to him and his lessons were double maths, English then lunch. Jake wasted no time in going to the library, taking two steps at a time up the stairs away from the hustle and bustle of the children spilling out from every classroom, relieved to be set free for a little while.

 The library had a great smell to it, Jake had to stand and think for a moment before he could pin point what it was then it came to him.. the books, they had their own scent. Some were new, some old, some bound by leather and the combined mixture was a good smell. Jake liked it. It was beautifully quiet and calm, he had never really spent time here before but now he took his time looking around. There was so much to read, so much to learn. There were adventure books, fact, autobiographies, just rows upon rows on wall to wall shelves of books. Jake realised he had found another favourite place and took his time selecting a book about planets.

"Oh that's a good one. I- I've r-r-read that" A nervous looking boy about the same age as Jake stammered next to him. He had round glasses and short brown hair, he stood fiddling with his fingers "A-are you in the l-l-lunchtime club too?"

Jake nodded

"Oh, g-g-g-good. I thought I was the o-o-o-only one"

There was an awkward silence as the boy waited for Jake to say something. Jake looked down, concentrating on the cover of the book.

"ohh, Ok. W-w-w-w ell e-e-enjoy the b-b-book"

Jake gave an awkward smile and waved goodbye to show he wasn't being rude but he just hadn't known what to say. No-one had really tried to talk to him like that before, or if they had he hadn't been listening because the classrooms were too busy and noisy.

Jake sat down with his book and lost himself in the words, the pictures were incredible, it felt like no time at all had passed before the bell sounded for the afternoon lessons to begin.

"The p-p-pictures are really g-great i-i-in that b-b-book aren't they"

Jake nodded, sliding it back in to place.

"I-i-im Tom"

Silence again

"I-I-It's ok. I know y-y-y-you're Jake. Y-y-you don't talk. I-i-i-I try not to talk too m-m-m-much either b-b-because they t-t-tease me"

Jake knew what that was like and he tried to show sympathy in his face.

"A-a-a-anyway, see you t-t-tomorrow?"

Jake nodded, smiling.

"Ok b-b-bye"

Tom and Jake put their hands up in a wave, picked up their school bags and went to their classes. Jake had science which he really liked. All in all it was a good day and for the first time this school year he had even made a friend.. he thought. Tom didn't seem to mind that Jake didn't speak so maybe it didn't need to be difficult.

The rest of the week was good too. In drama class Miss Laindon asked Jake at the beginning if he would like to join in or help her with her scripts. He shook his head at joining in and nodded at helping. She showed him to the little office again where he had to highlight different peoples lines in different colours. He enjoyed doing that and worked meticulously through, making sure the green highlighter was only used for that character all the way through the script then started again with the pink one for the different character, then yellow, then blue, then orange. He was just about finished when Miss Laindon came through the door after the bell had sounded.

"Wow Jake, you've done a fine job here! Thank you. I must say this really is a big help you know. You have saved me a lot of work and you're contributing to the play as well." She smiled " You are a great organiser you really are" She gathered up the papers he had already done and placed them carefully in one of her many bags she always seemed to carry around. "If you would like to, you can get a little more involved in the play with some of the lists I need to make and circulate around to the performers?"

Jake nodded enthusiastically, this would be the first time he had got involved in anything like this, he didn't like the actual play but he loved the story and he was super organised too. For Miss Laindon to recognise his abilities to help in a different way was brilliant, he couldn't stop smiling on the way home.

Charlie was still on his mind, people had begun to talk about him at school. Would he be back on Monday after another weeks suspension or would he be expelled this time? None of them knew what Jake knew. He wondered what had happened, where Charlie was now, what happened with his mum. He asked his Mum those questions but she didn't know and said they probably never would but they had done what was best for Charlie and they had to be content with that.

With the summer break growing nearer every day, everyone was looking forward to the holidays. There had been a lot of changes at school for Jake, he still found a lot of it difficult but he was finding ways around the difficult stuff; certain teachers were helping him now too, he had his library at lunchtime he could go to, to escape and him and Tom often exchanged books about planets and space, Jake thought that maybe one day he would be able to use his voice with him, Tom stuttered a lot less around Jake too, he said it was because Jake didn't try to rush him to get his words out so he was more relaxed. Then there was Miss Laindon; Jake used to hate her lessons in the beginning, it was the cause of many meltdowns causing Jake to be the centre of attention. Attention he didn't want and that was when the teasing really started, then the bullying from Charlie. But now he helped her organise the plays by getting the scripts together and highlighting the lines for everyone, making lists for costumes and props.

 Mrs Pittman really encouraged Jake with his writing too and said he was doing really well, she had had a meeting with Jakes mum .. something about provision they said and Jake had to fill out an "all about me" form. He didn't understand it at first but after she explained it to him, he liked the idea. It was to show other teachers how to help him have his best days at school, he had never been asked that question before so he took his time and chose a template out of many different ones they showed him of the planets, he put his picture at the top and he was able to put on there what he was good at, what he liked and also what he felt he needed help with, there was a space on how things could be better for him. Through filling it out he was able to tell his teachers how he really felt for the first time and they had a meeting but Jake didn't want to go. Since then, 5 minutes before each lesson finished a timer went off with the teacher and Jake was able to gather his things to be the first out and make his way to the next lesson, that way he avoided all the crowds and was never late to his classes. PE was still a struggle, but the teacher seemed a little more understanding and got Jake helping out with the equipment more, when it did get loud in the hall he was allowed to go and sit in the changing rooms or he could run laps around the field so he still got his fitness the coach said. They were still working things out they said, but Jake felt calmer and happier than he ever had at school.

Charlie hadn't been around for three weeks, everyone was convinced he was expelled by now. So on Monday morning when Jake walked in to school and saw him standing there with his usual hoard of friends that always did his bidding his stomach felt like it fell to his knees. Jake rushed quickly past. Could he know it was him that told? Would he hate him even more now? Jake felt sick all morning and could hear all the whispers constantly about Charlie being back.

Jake was in the middle of trying to get to his next lesson before the bell went when he bumped in to Mrs Pittman.

"Oh Jake, I'm so glad I caught you. There has been a flood in the library toilets and they have had to close it today I'm afraid. I'm so sorry but today the library is out of bounds until they clean it all up, fingers crossed it will be open tomorrow"

Jake nodded, his throat drying up, that means Charlie would find him. Mrs Pittman hurried off and he was left in the hall wondering how he could stay out of sight.

After his French lesson at lunch time Jake had decided he would go as far back in the school field as he could and eat his sandwiches there, there was a Weeping willow tree he could hide behind. He had stayed in the toilets all break time scared of seeing Charlie and how Charlie would react to him.

He wasted no time in getting over to the willow tree at lunch time so as not to be seen and he wondered where Tom would spend his break time today but didn't want to risk looking for him. The sun beat down on Jakes neck and he closed his eyes doing his breathing exercise to calm himself.

"Oh look who it is! It's mute boy! Haven't seen you in ages, where you been hiding?" It was James, one of Charlies friends who always joined in with Charlie when he picked on someone. James was tall for his age, covered in freckles and had a shock of ginger hair. He took the mickey out of everyone he could, but while Charlie wasn't around, James had been a lot quieter Jake noticed.

"Come on! Speak up! Its rude not to answer when you're spoken to" James leaned over Jake menacingly. Jake was scared, Charlie wasn't with him but he must have told him what Jake did and they were both looking for him. Jake braced himself, he thought maybe James would hit him, or maybe he would just pick on him until he got bored and then go away. One thing was for sure, wherever James was, Charlie would be soon after.

"OI!" Jake flinched as they heard a shout "LEAVE HIM ALONE!"

James spun round and Jake looked up in shock. It was Charlie!

"What?" James looked completely confused "But —"

"I said leave him alone or you got me to deal with"

"Alright Charlie, I just thought-"

"Well you thought wrong didn't ya"

Jake watched as James skulked away, clearly feeling embarrassed at being told off by Charlie in front of everyone. As usual when Jake was about to be picked on, a crowd seemed to appear out of nowhere to watch and most of them were probably thankful it wasn't them.

Charlie stood there until James had walked off and the crowd dispersed, Jake wandered what was going to happen next. Charlie had his head down, his hands in his pockets. He kicked the ground a few times before he spoke.

"I know it was you, you know" Charlie said.

Jakes head snapped up, his breathing quickened.

"I saw you in the car, I know you saw"

Silence. It seemed to go on forever, Jake didn't know where to look or what to expect next.

"They were gonna expel me, they couldn't decide what to do" Charlie looked at the floor still "Then they said it would be good for me to have some kind of normality" Charlie rolled his eyes at the word normality. "But my new foster family is nice so I suppose I'd better not screw it up"

Charlie stood there for a minute longer, kicking the ground again "See you around" He began walking off then stopped and turned. He looked right at Jake this time.

"Oh, and Jake?"

Jake looked up, their eyes met and Charlie smiled. A genuine smile Jake had never seen before. It made him look a lot nicer.

"Thanks"

229

CHAPTER SIXTEEN

"Mum where's my wellies? Can't find them anywhere and I'm meeting Zoe in an hour" Sarah was half inside the cupboard under the stairs, pulling everything out that resembled any kind of shoe.

"You're not my welly, you're not my welly. Aaarrgh where are youuuu?!"

"Sarah for goodness sake look at the mess you're making!" Rebekah came through from the kitchen with a coffee in one hand and Sarah's wellies in the other.

"My wellies! You found them! Where were they?"

"By the back door where you left them." Rebekah smiled

"Thanks Mum" Sarah grabbed the wellies and began to walk away

"Excuse me, where do you think you're going?" Rebekah asked pointedly looking at all the shoes and boots Sarah had pulled from the cupboard in the hunt for her wellies.

"To finish getting ready, I still have to brush my hair, choose what dolls are coming, prepare some snacks.."

"All very important but first you can clean up your mess"

"Oh right. Ok" Sarah got to work sorting the cupboard out again and Rebekah sighed, taking her coffee back in to the kitchen. It was 8 a.m. Saturday morning and Sarah was meeting one of her friends on the field near home. This was a new friend and she happened to live close by, her brother knew Jake and he was coming too. It was a different way for them to spend their Saturday and Sarah was excited. They were taking a blanket to sit on because the grass was so wet after three days of rain (the reason for the wellies).

"Jake are you ready or what?" Sarah called upstairs.

"Sarah we've got ages yet. Chill out will you"

"I'm just getting ready and you should do the same. Have you had breakfast yet? I have"

Jake came downstairs dressed in his jeans and t shirt, carrying 3 space books; his latest ones. He knew Tom hadn't seen these yet and he wanted to show him some of the pictures, they were really cool.

"What's Zoe's brother's name again?" Sarah asked Jake.

"Tom"

"Right" She grinned as Jake sat down and poured out a bowl of honey hoops

"This is so exciting! How cool you know Tom and I know his sister! Zoe and I can run off and play and you two can be book worms together"

Jake rolled his eyes at Sarah with a mouthful of cereal.

"You know what I mean!" She nudged him in the ribs causing him to cough out some of his breakfast.

"It is cool though isn't it" Sarah stood next to him, eyes shining bright, hair all over the place. One hand on her beloved wellies and the other holding Betty. "To meet some friends together I mean"

Jake nodded "Yeah it is pretty cool" Jake felt happy, he never thought he would be meeting a friend on a weekend, but him and Tom had become friends. Sometimes Jake even spoke, but that had taken a while and Tom never made a big deal whether he did or didn't, he was just there as a friend and didn't judge. Same as Jake didn't rush Tom when he had something to say and couldn't stop stuttering his words. But they both loved space, nature and books. When Zoe had come round for an afternoon one day, Tom had walked her over and Jake was surprised to see him at the door; he had come in and Jake had shown him his room. They had swapped numbers so Jake could text and they had organised getting together today.

"You need to hurry up though, I mean come on!"

"Sarah you have plenty of time. Leave Jake alone to eat his breakfast will you?" Rebekah put her hands on Sarah's shoulders and walked her out of the kitchen "While you are waiting ever so patiently there is a bedroom upstairs with your name on it... literally that needs tidying up"

Sarah sighed loudly "Fine" before racing upstairs.

"Does she ever do anything slowly?" Rebekah shook her head and sat down with Jake at the table. Rebekah was still in her dressing gown, her familiar favourite coffee cup with the huge crack in it which Jake could have sworn it had gotten bigger, and smudges of mascara under her eyes where she must have forgotten to take it off before she went to bed last night.

"You ok?" She asked Jake, a small smile on her lips.

"Yeah, I am"

Rebekah looked thoughtful; she sipped her coffee, Jake loved the smell of her coffee, it was different to other coffee smells but when he smelt her type of coffee occasionally it always made him think of mum.

"You've come a long way Jake you know"

"What do you mean?" Jake was confused he hadn't gone anywhere.

"I mean things have changed for you haven't they" She took his hand "In a good way and slowly they are getting better. I can't tell you how proud I am of you, of everything you do. How hard you've pushed yourself even when it's been really, really difficult. You've done it"

 Jake understood now. He still didn't speak much at school but the odd yes or no to a teacher when it was just them was a start and a huge step Mum said. He had really helped Miss Laindon with the school play arrangements and wanted him to assist her in the next one from the start; Jake loved helping her, he felt useful and he was good at organising. It felt good for someone to notice the things he was good at and the teachers seemed a bit more understanding too. They had all been given a copy of his "all about me" which at first Jake felt a bit embarrassed about but when he realised how much it had helped them to know what he needed he was glad of it.

 Charlie was a lot quieter at school now too. They would never be friends but at least Charlie was no longer Jake's bully. Charlie wanted to stay in school and he actually behaved himself (Not completely) he was still getting in trouble for things but small things and was a lot less angry all the time.

 Jake and Tom would eat their lunch quickly together on the bench outside the building of the library then hurry upstairs to look through different books and exchange facts. Tom would share his and practice not stuttering by talking really slowly and Jake would point to an extract In a book he wanted Tom to read. It worked.

Jake nodded, he was actually happy. He started this school year not knowing how he would ever get through it and now he was making it work, he enjoyed his lessons and had even made a friend. There were some bad days when things got too much, too much noise, confusion and busyness made him shut down in to himself mum said; Jake never really knew what that meant, he just seemed to find himself somewhere else rocking and holding his ears. Those were not good days but the teachers were starting to notice the signs and began to step in before he got too upset. They introduced a quiet space for Jake for those moments and he noticed it wasn't long before other kids were using it too. Other kids that got upset by too much noise. He thought it was just him; that he was weird, but it wasn't just him, he wasn't weird at all.... just a bit different. The quiet space was next to the art room; it had comfy chairs and a couple of tables and art supplies and that was it. Jake found drawing his emotions really helpful, it helped him express himself when the words wouldn't come.

"Have you not finished yet?!" Sarah bounded down the stairs two at a time holding Betty and Daisy her two favourite dolls, she was already wearing her rain mac, her hair now brushed. She was ready to go.

"I've just got to brush my teeth, be five minutes" Jake put his bowl in the sink and headed upstairs, he could hear his Mum asking Sarah if she had actually tidied her room and reminding her that she still had 30 minutes before their friends would be there. He knew what books he was taking along with him to show Tom and his boots were by the back door as well, he needed five minutes away from Sarah's chatter though. He was excited to see his friend and so glad Sarah had one too. The thought occurred to him that she could have had friends over any time she had wanted, seeing her at school showed him that but she loved her big brother and spending time with him, she also knew he hadn't had a friend before Tom and didn't want to leave him out. The thought that she had done that for Jake made him love her even more, she had put her own self aside for him.

Seeing her so excited was proof to Jake she had wanted to spend time with friends outside of school on a weekend for a long time, he was surprised he hadn't seen it before.

By the time Tom and Zoe knocked, Sarah was beside herself and so impatient.

"They're here!" Sarah squealed, jumping up to open the door immediately.

Tom and Zoe came through to say hi to Rebekah before they went off. Rebekah had gotten dressed by then and had started on the usual cleaning routine in the kitchen. Tom was dressed in jeans and t shirt like Jake, trainers and had a jacket in case of the rain, Zoe had a pink dress, wellie boots and a back pack. Two dolls heads poked out the back, she was holding her rain mac, it was pink like her dress.

"Hello" Zoe said

"H-H-Hello" Tom stuttered

"Hi there you two. I'm Rebekah, good to meet you both" Rebekah smiled.

"Well, we are ready. Shall we go? We know a lovely place don't we Jake? But there is a great field. I've got some snacks and a blanket too. I bet the grass is really wet. You ready Jake?"

Jake nodded. Rebekah gave them both a kiss and told them to have fun but to be back by 1. She watched as the four of them made their way out the back door and out the back gate to the field. Her heart swelling with pride, tears of happiness in her eyes to see them with their friends, especially Jake. She could see Sarah talking nonstop as usual but Zoe was chatting away just as fast too. They were laughing and running, skipping and throwing their dolls up in the air, catching them and whooping, happy to be running free in the field. Rebekah looked up at the sky, it was warm and muggy but the thick dark clouds threatened rain. She hoped it would hold off for them, they had had so much rain the last few days.

CHAPTER SEVENTEEN

"This I-I-Is the P-p-page" Tom opened his book and showed Jake the picture of Saturn "I-It says the sm-mall p-particles are almost all m-made of ice" Tom pointed to the rings around Saturn, Jake knew this already but loved sharing the books with Tom. Tom spoke very slowly and stuttered less.

Jake nodded, studying the picture. Sarah and Zoe were shrieking with laughter and playing with their dolls. They had picked handfuls of daisies, had begun making daisy chains for each other and were already muddy. Tom and Jake had found a dry patch of grass under an acorn tree and were flicking through the pages of Toms book.

"Aaagh rain!" Sarah and Zoe jumped up, gathering their dolls and blanket as big plops of rain started slowly, then steadily until it was falling down hard. The girls ran to the acorn tree as fast as they could but were soaked by the time they got there.

"Nooooo" Sarah looked so sad and disappointed "I don't want to have to go home yet"

Jake put his arm around her, trying to dry her off a bit before handing her, her rain mac. He didn't want to go home either, none of them did. Then he had an idea. He tapped Sarah on the shoulder and pointed towards the woods.

"Great idea Jake! We will stay dry under the trees. Come on everyone!"

They quickly gathered up their things and all ran over to the woods getting wet as they went. The rain spattered over all of them making them shriek and run faster, by the time they got to the woods they were all out of breath, laughing and soaking wet. The earthy smell met Jake immediately. The trees protected them from the rain like giant arms, It wasn't cold; still quite muggy, so they took off their rain coats each finding a branch to hang them on to dry out.

The rain continuously tip tapped on the branches and leaves, some finding their way through and plopping on to the soft leaves on the ground but mostly it was dry.

"Wow this is ace! I can't believe we've never been here before !" Zoe exclaimed

"Yeah it's b-beautiful" Tom agreed.

Jake and Sarah exchanged knowing looks and smiled, silently sharing their secret with each other.

"What shall we do?" Zoe asked, beginning to explore the woods

"Let's make a den!" Sarah cried

They all got to work together finding thick fallen branches to make their den, using one of the trees as a base to lean them all on and built it round in a triangle shape. It took them ages getting it just right and Sarah and Zoe had an idea to make one just for the dolls too. They found some branches with leaves on and placed them on top.

Jake and Sarah took extra care to make sure they didn't spoil any mushrooms or step on any creatures. They had a much greater respect for the woods than they did before they had met the fairies.

Gathering leaves for their floor and rolling big logs towards the den for outside seating they all had a wonderful time. The girls ate their snacks in the den; chattering constantly and giggling, while the boys sat on the outside log eating theirs. It was getting close to 1 now, the time had gone so quickly.

Jake noticed Sarah looking towards the tree stump, then she looked at her dolls and seemed lost in thought. Jake hadn't dared look as yet and knew what she had been thinking.

Zoe and Tom had started getting their coats on

"Hey you ok?" Jake asked while they were out of ear shot.

Sarah nodded "Do you think they will understand"

"Of course. I think they will be happy for us" Jake put his arm around Sarah "Especially Rowan and Heather too"

"You think so?" She smiled then

"I really do" Jake nodded

"Maybe we will go back one day"

"Maybe we will"

Their time in the woods had come to an end, they needed to head home now to be back on time. It had been full of fun and laughter and friendship.

They had explored so much of it and there was still so much more to explore for next time they had all agreed. Things he and Sarah had missed.

All four of them began walking back slowly; not wanting their morning to end. It had stopped raining now, Jake and Tom carrying their books and Sarah and Zoe swinging their dolls. They were just about to leave the woods when Sarah stopped dead in her tracks.

"Wait! I'll be back in a minute" She ran back inside the woods.

Jake frowned, wondering what she was doing, he followed her but hung back a little. Sarah was kneeling over by the tree trunk and setting Betty down next to it so she was sitting upright. She kissed her and said something then ran back towards Jake.

"For Rowan?" He asked.

"Yeah" Sarah nodded. "But how do you think they will pull it through?"

Jake thought for a moment "I think they will find a way"

When they came back out Tom and Zoe were waiting for them.

"Hey! Where is Betty?" Zoe asked.

"I've left her behind to have some adventures" Sarah answered

Jake put his arm around Sarah, proud of her and feeling happy.

"But isn't she your absolute favourite doll Sarah?!" Zoe was surprised Sarah could leave her behind.

"She is. That's why I want her to have amazing adventures" Sarah smiled, looked up at Jake and winked. Jake smiled back and the four of them slowly walked towards home.

The end.

Author: Claire Lamb

Illustrator: Frankie Lamb

Printed in Great Britain
by Amazon